# THE DAILY CHRONICLES OF
# *DAKOTA*
# *ELLISON*

Sharon Butler-Charles

Published by Pen Culture Solutions   04/16/2024

Pen Culture Solutions
1-888-727-7204 (USA)
1-800-950-458 (Australia)
support@penculturesolutions.com

# The Daily Chronicles of Dakota Ellison

# CHAPTER 1

Amusty stench soured the sultry night air. A trail of clothing was strewn about the mahogany hardwood floor leading to Dakota's bedroom. Dakota Ellison, is a successful entrepreneur who lay draped across her bed, recovering from the last romantic suitor of three years, who upended her life and emotional stability like a tsunami on steroids. "I hate you Rayal," she determined, as she wept quietly while scrolling through the many images of the two of them, during happier days on her mobile phone. Dakota's eyes were filled with tears as she was momentarily interrupted by a buzzing sound coming from the kitchen. Dakota lived alone in a large upscale high rise condominium building located in the downtown district of Charlotte, North Carolina. As she quietly crept towards the buzzing sound, she soon came face to face with the culprits. A host of flies and larvae had invaded several cartons of food that lay naked in the trash bin. Many of the larvae had cascaded from the trash bin onto the floor. Shocked, Dakota uttered loudly, "How did this happen?" She went on to add, "Where is my head?" Gazing disappointedly at the infested trash bin, she quickly removed the trash and larvae, taking care to disinfect the entire affected area. With the larvae moving about under her soiled hand, she muttered to herself, "This is disgusting."

She then immediately dragged the plastic bin to the dumpster located on the lower level of her condominium complex.

After returning to her unit, looking in the mirror that had been strategically placed in her vestibule, Dakota noticed how pathetic she looked. She began to examine the clumped and incredibly old mascara that had laid claim to her eyelashes, lashes that had seen better days. Her mascara and pasty makeup captured the trail of tears that stained her pretty brown skin. Looking intently at herself in the mirror she stated, "I deserve better, and I will do better," she committed to the very pitiful image in the mirror. Dakota continued, "This will be the last time I allow any man to use me and deceive me, ever again. I know better and I will do better."

As Dakota secured the door to her condominium unit and began advancing towards her disheveled bedroom for a much-needed shower, she was grabbed from behind. Her cries for help are muffled by a strong muscular hand that covered her mouth and wrestled her slender athletic frame onto the hard, unforgiving floor. Dakota writhed beneath her assailant, but to no avail, her attempts were unmatched by the intruder's powerful dominance. "Stop fighting," the intruder asked her softly. "I will not hurt you, I need for you to cooperate, but keep your eyes closed, or else you will be sorry. Do you understand?" Exhausted and breathless, Dakota acquiesces to the requestor.

As Dakota remained trapped under her accoster, she could hear his breathing and counted in her head every bulge protruding from his muscular frame onto her back. As the accoster rested atop her, she could feel the searing heat from his nostrils against the right side of her face and neck. With her eyes still closed, and her heart still pounding, the feeling of terror that she once felt is immediately replaced by feelings of arousal and passion. The muscular accoster began to whisper in her ear, "Is this what you want? Dakota's groans became more labored and began to reverberate around her quaint abode. Sensing her full participation, the intruder removed his hands from her soft full mouth and with her eyes still closed, the intruder married his loins to hers, rendering Dakota a victim to her own full participation with a total stranger. Unashamedly, Dakota completely allowed herself to experience the illicit invasion of her intruder and somehow reciprocated in ways that are too numerous to recant. Dakota had never experienced such bliss and wanted nothing more than to have this encounter last forever. Just then, the sound of what seemed like police sirens were swarming the condominium complex. Dakota begins to panic realizing the police have now swarmed her building and are probably looking for her accoster. "Don't open your eyes, or you'll be sorry," the accoster reminds her. However, the police sirens are deafening and the fear she once had of her accoster has again returned. Dakota could hear the footsteps of the officers making their way to her unit, but remembering the instructions from her accoster, she remained paralyzed in utter fear. Without warning, there was a loud thud at her door, "BOOM, BOOM, BOOM, BOOM" and on impulse she screamed and opened her eyes. Dakota sprang out of bed from a deep sleep and yelled, "Oh, God, I really need help!! Not another horrific, disgusting nightmare!"

# CHAPTER 2

**M**y Story is extremely complicated. My name is Dakota Ellison. I am a single African American woman, 41 years of age, with no children. I am a successful Banker at one of the largest financial institutions on the east coast and love my profession. However, for the past 3 years, I have been suffering with recurring, disgusting dreams that dwarf my romantic reality, and are terrifyingly taboo. I'm not in the least bit concerned about these dreams, because after all, they are just dreams. Period. My dating has been a challenge, because I do not like being compared to other women, nor do I like to compete for the affection of men that I may be attracted to. Therefore, my romantic life is somewhat nonexistent.

It is currently 6:45 a.m. on a Monday morning and I am exhausted from last night's dream and have exactly one hour to get myself in gear for work.

Lucky for me, I managed to arrive for work at 8:00 a.m. Mondays are usually busy, but that's ok, because it will keep me from having flashbacks about my most recent dream. I have not shared my dreams with anyone at this point, because I don't want to be judged. And besides, I always remind myself they are only dreams. Actually, I have my eye on a few prospects, but many of them are bank customers and I could absolutely lose my job if I dated bank customers, as it would be a conflict of interest, to say the least. Although it's against the bank policy, it's hard, because I feel a connection with a few of my gentlemen customers. In fact, during an occasion last week, I inadvertently wrote my personal mobile number on my business card and handed it to two of my male customers. I'm not sure if they're married, or not, but they never called, so I'll assume they are not interested. Anyway, the bank just implemented a new banking system, and I am on the hook to assist with the facilitation of the training. The training will take place over a four-week period. I'm really looking forward to it.

After leaving the office today, I ran an errand and bumped

into a gentleman by the name of Gregory Wayland, who just so happens to live in my condominium complex. Gregory asked if I was still working in banking. I had given him my business card one morning when we were both leaving for the office. I explained to Gregory that I was still working in banking, and we proceeded to exchange niceties. He asked if we could go out for coffee to discuss a potential business endeavor that he had in mind. As luck would have it, he handed me his business card and suggested we get together sometime this week, or as soon as possible, as he was looking for a financial institution to fund his project. Of course, I obliged him and agreed to reach out to him, especially since I had a small crush on him going back three years. Gregory has beautiful brown eyes and a very gorgeous smile. His teeth are eerily straight, and his eyes are nothing short of intoxicating. I will most definitely be reaching out to Mr. Gregory, sooner than later, especially since we live in the same condominium complex. There are one hundred and ten units in the Ellington Estates Condominium Complex (EECC), which is where Gregory and I reside, and own our own units. I am fortunate to have secured my unit before the Complex was completed. You see, my dad was the lead developer on the project, so it all worked out in my favor. My condominium is located on the tenth floor, unit 1010. Gregory's condominium is located on the third floor, unit 311.

I cannot believe it's already 7:45 p.m. and I am just arriving home after another very long day at the bank. I will probably turn in early, especially since I will need to arrive super early for work tomorrow. I am sort of an overachiever, it's in my blood. My dad is an established developer and has always worked seven days a week. His days seem to never end. He is a wonderful provider and a devoted family-oriented person, but his work is and will forever be, his top priority.

# CHAPTER 3

My goal is to be in bed by 10:00 p.m. I pray I sleep well. It's 2:00 a.m. and I'm still wide awake. I just checked my messages and saw an incoming text from Gregory. The text message was sent to me at 11:00 p.m. Gregory said he was happy to have run into me today. He also invited me over to his place for an early dinner this evening, at 6:00 pm. I'm completely flattered, but not surprised by his invitation. I knew he wanted me from the way his eyes flirted with me during our brief encounter. He wasn't looking at me, but I could tell he really wanted to. The way he handed me his business card was another sign that if we were ever alone, I would be in big trouble. I like trouble, especially when it's anticipated. Well, it is now 4:30 a.m. and I am waiting for the right time to confirm my date with Greg.

Oh, crap! It's 7:00 a.m. and I've overslept again! This is not how I want to start my Tuesday! This will be the second day in a row that I will be struggling to make it into work on time. I will need to order a rideshare service to get into work on time. Taking a rideshare will also give me time to decide how to respond back to Greg.

It is difficult to contain my excitement. It's 7:45 a.m. and I am now heading to work in a Rideshare service, which is only a 7-to-10-minute commute from my condo. I will text Gregory right now to confirm our dinner date for tonight, but I will move the time back by 30 minutes, so it appears I have something going on in my personal life and do not appear too eager, too available, or too desperate. Just like magic, Gregory has already confirmed our 6:30 p.m. dinner and says he is looking forward to having me over this evening.

I have got to get my act together. I am just arriving at work, a mere five minutes prior to my 8 a.m. start time!! This is so unlike me. I'm a bit embarrassed to arrive at work on the heels of my official start time. I know my naysayers will be all over this. While checking my office mail bin, I overheard a few of my colleagues giggling about me arriving "just in time" for work. I must say, it's a bad look, especially since I am the VP of Personal Banking Services. I've set the bar high here at Algonquin Personal and Commercial Banking and Financial Services. During my 10-year tenure with the organization, I routinely arrive one hour in advance of my start time, not to mention, I've managed to maintain a perfect attendance record. Again, I am an overachiever, so arriving on time is a problem and super embarrassing.

It's 1:00 p.m. and I can barely concentrate on my work, because I've been constantly planning my outfit for my dinner date with Gregory this evening. It has been a very long time since I've gone out on a date, so I want to wear something special. I have a few cute pieces in mind, but I will just need to try them on once I arrive home. Since Gregory and I live in the same condo complex, I should be all set for time.

I am completely ahead of schedule. I have already showered and have decided to wear a black fitted jersey, with a gold, leather pencil skirt. I decided to forego wearing nylons, because I really like wearing my black sexy peep toe sandals. Besides, my legs are in great shape. I also like the way the oil that I apply to my legs shimmers when I walk. My cross training has paid off if I must say so myself.

I just received another text from Gregory. This time he said he is checking to see how my day is going and to inform me that he's all set for our dinner date this evening. He must be as excited about tonight as I am. It's only 5:45 p.m. and I am completely dressed, but I won't arrive at his unit until 6:30 p.m., promptly. I am wearing a very pretty fragrance. I really hope Gregory likes it.

# CHAPTER 4

It is now 6:25 p.m. and I just texted Gregory to tell him that I am heading down to his condo unit. I am a bit nervous, but happy I decided against wearing nylons. I am now in Gregory's unit. Incidentally, as I exited the elevator, he was waiting for me dripping in sexy and flashing his amazing, super white teeth. Gregory's condo unit is amazing. His window treatments are high-end, and his home furnishings have all the trappings for a night of romance.

"Dakota, thank you for coming," Gregory said. "Absolutely," I said with a soft smile. Gregory proceeded to give me a tour of his place and then as we returned to the dining area, he began to ask about my day. I could see he was fishing for words, but it didn't matter, because my eyes were locked on to his lips and his sexy long legs that seemed to extend for miles. I didn't eat much during dinner, largely because the protein on the menu was Grilled Salmon and since I am a vegan, I only ate my veggies, which consisted of a baked potato and carrots, which were tasty. Truth be told, I was only interested in another type of protein that wasn't necessarily on the menu, but a product he could produce.

After dinner, Gregory shared his proposed business model with me and eagerly shared a hardcopy of the PowerPoint document that he had used in an earlier presentation of his proposed endeavor along with his loan application. Gregory went on to ask if I could look at his business plan and provide feedback, to ensure his application filing process would meet the criteria for financing at the bank. Hesitantly, I agreed to look over his business plan, fully acknowledging that involvement of any kind on my part would be a conflict of interest, especially since he was looking to finance his endeavor through my employer.

Gregory was pleased that I had agreed to assist him with the review process of his business plan and without warning leaned in and gave me a firm embrace. We were seated side by side on the sofa, so the embrace was a bit awkward. I asked Gregory how soon he needed my feedback, even though I had no intention of reviewing any of the material, but he smelled so good, and I just wanted to make small talk to keep him engaged. Just then, Gregory placed his hand firmly on top of mine. His warm massive hand lay atop of my hand like a deliberate protector and his eyes locked onto mine like a heat seeking missile that had discovered its intended target. "Dakota," he said, "thank you for agreeing to spend your evening with me and for your help with this project, this really means a lot to me." Gregory handed me a folder that contained his completed business plan, the completed loan application and relevant documentation. Gregory went on to add that he would email me an electronic copy of the business plan in case I wanted to make any edits and we could discuss my feedback, accordingly. Gregory's lip continued to move, but I don't remember anything he said after that, because I was thinking in my head how nice it would be to kiss him, right then, right there, right now. With my hand still completely surrendered under his, I somehow felt safe, wanted, and even excited about what was happening at that moment. I, from time to time, could feel Gregory's tender grasps gently squeezing my hand beneath his strong, masculine, tender compresses. Feeling a rush over my entire body, I immediately asked Gregory if I could excuse myself and use the restroom. Just then, Gregory leaned into me and said, "Of course, follow me." As Gregory stood up to escort me in the direction of the restroom, I on purpose brushed against him and then pretended I didn't realize what I had just done. While in the bathroom, with the water in the face bowl running for the sole purpose of drowning out my intentions, I took the opportunity to check myself out in the mirror and then proceeded to look around his bathroom to get a sense of what my potential husband may be into.

After riffling through the cabinets in his bathroom, I flushed the toilet for no reason, quickly washed my hands and then exited the bathroom. When I returned to the living room area he was still standing. As I walked towards him, I could see he was checking me out from head to toe. I didn't mind, because the body oil that I use on my legs was still fresh and working overtime to accentuate my supple brown skin. I told him I should be getting back to my unit, because it was getting late, and I had an early start in the morning. Gregory walked me to the door, but not before thanking me again and pulling me in for a soft kiss on my eager mouth. I really wanted to overpower him and make him my captive at that moment, but instead I blushed and quickly exited his unit.

I was so overcome with excitement that I nearly fainted, as I made my way to the elevator. I needed some alone time to process what had just happened and couldn't wait to sort it all out once I returned to my condo. As I approached my unit, I quickly realized I had left my purse, keys, and cell phone back at Gregory's condo. Hurriedly, I made a mad dash for the elevator and quickly returned to his unit, but before I could reach for the bell, he opened the door. There he stood, dripping in nature's finest, Mandingo chocolate with barely a button affixed to hold back the avalanche of muscles that were destined to break free from his loincloth. "Did you leave something behind?" He said. Nervously, I stated, "Yes, I left my purse along with my keys and cell phone." At that point he asked me to step inside to locate my belongings. I apologized for my oversight and assured him that I would be in and out. As I advanced towards the area where I was seated, I immediately spotted my small purse on the sofa where we both had been seated. However, my keys and cell phone were not present. That's when I saw Gregory quietly standing across from me with his hands in his front pant pockets. Suddenly, his lips began to part and with a soft voice he stated, "Maybe you should check my pockets." By this time, his face was expressionless, and his beautiful brown skin was

working in unison with the soft
ambient lighting in his cozy
condo. Greg's hair was close
cropped, and every curl had its
own resting place. Considering
Gregory's offer, I said to myself,
"What a beautiful Black man
you are Mr. Gregory ", but I was
careful not to let those words
escape my desperate lips and
remained calm, collected, and
determined to stay focused. I
giggled and assured Gregory
I needn't be going through his
pockets because I may leave with
more than my belongings. He
began walking towards me and
standing directly in front of
me asked me to take my things
from his pockets. By this time,
he had removed his hands from
his pockets, and I could see the

oblong print of my phone in his left pocket and the imprint of my many keys in his right pocket. Jokingly, I reached for his left pocket and began slowly working my hand down into his pocket. When I connected with my phone, I pulled it out and proceeded to work my hands into his right pocket. This time it required more work because the keys were a bit deeper in his pocket. As I worked my way down his pocket, I intercepted what felt like pure perfection. The large mass interrupted my ability to safely navigate to reach my keys. As I was about to retract my hand, Gregory held my wrist in place and asked me to go deeper. His straight teeth were now at eye level and by now his chest was close to my face. I sank my left hand deep into Gregory's pocket pretending to be unfazed by the obstruction in his right pocket. Without notice, I plunged my left hand deeper into his pocket, pressing against an anonymous tenant that posed an imminent threat to the success of me retrieving my keys from his ever so warm, snug pocket. As I slowly pulled my keys to freedom, we both stood there in utter silence for about ten seconds and then I looked up at him and said, "Thanks!" and ran out the door towards the elevator.

# CHAPTER 5

It is now 10:15 p.m. and I am very much wired from my dinner tonight with Gregory and I am also feeling a bit shook from my close encounter with Gregory. Exercise has always been my escape when I am feeling anxious, but tonight was special and I don't want to break the romantic spell from tonight. I need to savor the warm emotions from tonight's escapade with Gregory. I need to give my mind, body, and psyche permission to envelop all the beautiful possibilities that may never come to fruition. Therefore, I will not ruin the mood by working out. Instead, I'll retreat to some soft sultry music. Romantic Jazz and other similar genres have always been my escape when

I'm feeling a certain way and creates the perfect soundtrack for drowning out the sound of the motor from my large stainless-steel refrigerator that I can always count on to quietly serenade the atmosphere and provide the perfect vibe for the dust particles lay claim to my entertainment center. The dust is not that noticeable, but I will eventually get around to evicting the dust bunnies during my next cleaning spell.

I have already queued up my favorite playlist and will just wait for my much-needed calm to settle in. I really like Greg and tonight confirmed that we both are very much attracted to one another. Actually, I just got off the phone with Gregory. He said he was calling to make sure I arrived back at my condo safely. He also stated that he really enjoyed my company and wanted a tour of my apartment. Within minutes of me ending my call with him, he texted me to say he was at my door. I was super excited when I opened the door to find Gregory standing there more handsome than I had recalled. His cologne was masculine. His Jawline was strong, his body was athletic, and his intentions were crystal clear. "Thank you for inviting me in," Gregory stated in a soft, masculine voice, as he slowly crossed the threshold of my condo. My heart began to race and the heat from his presence permeated the entire room. Gregory's confidence was intoxicating. I closed the door behind my chocolate stallion and knew in that moment, tonight was going to be more than a casual visit.

With my favorite jazz playlist still queued up in the background, Gregory began to tell me how much he loved my condo. We advanced to the balcony, where the skyline was perfect on that clear night. Not to mention, the night air was so refreshing. In all honesty, I brought him out there, because I wanted to get as far away from my bedroom as possible. I had not been on a date in years, but that's not something he needed to know. It felt nice to have Gregory over, a man over. "I like the view from your balcony," he said. And that's when it happened. Gregory leaned in and kissed me. His hands nestled perfectly in the small of my back. His lips were silky and his mouth tenderly enveloped mine. I slowly wrapped my arms around his neck and thoroughly enjoyed the moment. He took my hand and led me back into the living room area of my condo. We made out for a while on the sofa, to the many melodies of my favorite, romantic, jazz playlist. Caught up in the moment, I asked Gregory if he wanted to spend the night. I don't recall him ever answering, I just remember him leaving my apartment at 5:30 a.m., the next day, because he kissed me on the shoulder before he left. The whole night was surreal.

# CHAPTER 6

Wednesday morning rolled in like a boulder charging down an unforgiving cliff. It is 6:17 a.m. and I am completely dragging from my night with Gregory. As I stand in the shower, I can still feel him near me and take comfort in knowing that the best parts of him are deposited deep within me. My night with Gregory was bittersweet, because I have never had a one-night stand, especially since it goes against who I am as an upstanding Christian woman, or at least that's what I used to be. Yet, here I am, in a situation that has left me questioning everything I've ever known about myself.

It is now 7:10 a.m., and I just arrived at my office. I made it a point to wear something a bit professional, but sexy, just in case Gregory calls me and wants to do lunch, or should I run into him in the lobby area of our condominium complex, after work.

Today has been a super productive day at the office. I successfully met all my deliverables, which means my client portfolio and my management team are happy. I routinely work through my lunch break, but I honestly was hoping to hear from Gregory. He's been on my mind all day and I can't seem to get our romantic dalliances from last night, off my mind. I shouldn't make more out of what happened between us last night, but somehow, I know I will. I'm sure Gregory is used to women falling for him, so what's one more? Anyway, it's now about 4:00 p.m., the end of my workday and I still have not heard from Gregory. How could I let myself fall to a guy who clearly could care less about me?

Well, since I am all caught up here at the office, I will head out in hopes of getting an earlier start tomorrow. As I was bidding my goodnights to my colleagues, and heading to the parking garage, my cell phone began to vibrate in my purse. "Please let it be Gregory," I utter in a soft voice." As I took my phone from my purse, I could clearly see it was Gregory calling me. "Hello?" I said. "Hi Dakota, it's Greg. How was your day?" he said. In that moment, Gregory's mesmerizing voice melted away any apprehension I had about him from my earlier thoughts. I immediately responded, "Hi Greg, it's so nice to hear your voice. My day was great! How was yours?" Somehow calling him Greg made me feel closer to him. At that time, I had located my vehicle and was seated in the driver's seat. Greg continued, "I hope I am part of the reason why you had such a great day at work. Did you think of me at all today?" Trying to control my excitement and with a soft voice I uttered, "Yes, I believe you already know that you have been on my mind since 5:30 a.m. this morning when you kissed me goodbye, right before you left my condo."

I began to chuckle nervously, when Greg interrupted me to ask if he could see me again tonight. He said he couldn't get me out of his head and asked if he could bring a vegan pizza to make up for the salmon, he served me the previous night when I visited his place.

Without giving it any thought, I heard myself say, "Sure, I would love to see you again tonight. What time should I expect you?" Greg responded, "Dakota, I would like to see you right now if I could. How about I arrive at 6:30 p.m., will that work for you?" Barely breathing, I told him any time after 6:30 p.m. would be fine and thanked him in advance for bringing the vegan pizza.

# CHAPTER 7

Greg arrived promptly at 6:27 p.m., three minutes earlier than he had requested. I interpreted this as a sign that he was in fact falling ridiculously hard for me and that was ok and exactly what I wanted. Greg's sweet lips were beautifully moist, puckered and calling my name. "Dakota, you look amazing tonight," he said, as he handed me the warm, delicious smelling vegan, cauliflower crust pizza and planted an unexpected peck on my unprepared, but willing lips. "Thank you, Greg," I said, in the most appreciative and loving tone that organically resonated from my being. I, on purpose wore a warm burnt orange, flirty, figure flattering, above the knee, shift dress. Tonight, would be special, so I wore my hair open, allowing my curls to frame my face and find their own resting place along my neck and back area, which will allow Greg's large fingers to roam deeply in my crown.

Greg's eyes felt like a blow torch on my delicate skin, as his loving glances branded every square inch of my frame. "I'm really hungry, Dakota," Greg said. The base in his voice was so prominent, soft, and tender that I nearly pounced on him for a second kiss, but I needed more intel to discern if his hunger was literal or figurative. "Yes, I am also very ravenous," I said as I offered him to wash his hands at the kitchen sink so we could bless the food and prepare to eat.

During dinner, Gregory talked for what seemed like hours about his project and as he rambled on, I sat there mesmerized by his masculinity, white teeth, and intelligence. Gregory went from one subject to the next, pouring out his heart to his future wife, me. Gregory never once asked for my input, but that was perfectly fine, because the more he talked the more I fell in love with him.

"Dakota, honey, I cannot thank you again for agreeing to look over my business plan and other related documents, prior to me submitting my packet and completed loan application to your lending institution for review and consideration." At that point it was clear that Gregory was there to discuss his future business endeavors with the bank and needed my assistance to critique his package, which also included his business loan application and relevant documentation. "Oh, sure, no problem. The pleasure is all mine. I will look at it tomorrow and get back to you in a few days with my feedback," I blurted out sweetly, knowing that it was untrue. I loved spending time with Gregory and would not do anything to jeopardize my romantic prospects with him, even if it meant me intentionally misleading him.

Well, as it turns out, Gregory was hungry, because he devoured three quarters of the pizza and drank two very large glasses of cranberry-apple juice, before announcing he would be retiring early to prepare for work in the morning. He walked himself to the door and blew me a kiss goodnight, but not before mouthing the words, "I'll see you tomorrow." Not wanting the evening to end, I begged him not to leave and rushed towards him, in a desperate attempt to extend our time together and in the absence of any dialogue, I fleeced him with my soft lips, removing every stitch of clothing that shrouded his chocolate mountain of absolute perfection. The passion between us was magnetic and due to the force of our passion, we both fell to the floor and began thrashing one another with unadulterated ecstasy. Our human vessels were synchronously entwined, until the universe rendered us breathless, speechless, and more in love than ever. Well, that's what happened in my head, at least. Ok, so what really happened was, I forced a fake smile to hide my disappointment and said, "Sure, let's catch up tomorrow, Greg."

# CHAPTER 8

Greg and I have been seeing each other for three months now and it feels amazing to be booed up. Greg is my boo!

About his business, I spent a good amount of time assuring Greg that the bank will finance his business endeavor, but what he doesn't know is that the paperwork and supporting documentation is still on my desk. I never submitted it. Sure, I told him his proposal is in process and is being reviewed, but I figure my stalling will give us more time to bond, more time to build our life. If he contacts the bank, I will pretend it's all a mistake and submit the proposal at that point.

I have waited my entire life to find a man like Greg and I

will do anything and everything humanely possible to keep him, including withholding the thing that will make him need me less. Greg completely trusts me, which I know will eventually fuel our relationship, securing our future.

By and large, I am a very honest person. In my past relationships, I did everything by the book. I was super transparent. Loved openly and revealed too much about thoughts, feelings and was truthful to a fault. But I am a bit jaded now and besides, love has a way of hijacking one's perspective, emotions, and spiritual vision. So, for now, I am going to ride this wave. Quitting is not an option.

It is now 1:11 a.m. and I haven't seen Greg in days. He

called me three days ago to ask if I had an update regarding the financial application and proposal. I told him I hadn't received an update and assured him I would keep him posted. Greg didn't stay on the phone for more than a minute and ended the call, but I am almost certain I heard a female voice in the distance. Wait, maybe I imagined that. Anyway, I am not a jealous person, so I won't bring it up with Greg when I see him again, because our time together is way too precious.

# CHAPTER 9

It has been a total of seven days since I've seen or heard from Greg. Due to the stress from his unexplained absence, I haven't slept or properly eaten in days and it's beginning to affect me physiologically, as well as my work.

The next day as I prepared for work, I decided to take the elevator downstairs to Greg's unit. Since I was the first person to enter the elevator on my level, I decided to position myself in the rear of the elevator to collect my thoughts, especially since I was extremely nervous. The elevator stopped at every floor and the closer I got to the floor where Greg's unit is located, the more nervous I became and the more

I "got in my head." My heart was racing a mile a minute and I was sure he would be excited to see me. I was certain that his absence was due to his work and family obligations. In fact, Greg once told me that he often visits his parents and spends a lot of time assisting with their affairs. That's the kind of man I want and need. Yes, a loving, kind family man. Greg. My boo. As the elevator approached each floor, the sound of the signal bell was nauseating and heightened my anxiety. Closing my eyes allowed me to focus on my impending encounter with my boo.

I tried to count the number of bell indications until we reached Greg's floor, but I lost count. It was like a vacuum. Suddenly,

I could smell Greg's presence standing before me. Greg had entered the elevator and leaned into me and softly whispered, "Good morning, beautiful." Greg proceeded to plant a soft wet kiss on my dry cracked lips and continued, "I've missed you and planned on coming by tonight, providing that's ok with you, Dakota." I was at a loss for words and nodded in agreement. I just wanted him to hold me and assure me that we were still good. Greg began to deeply kiss me in ways he had never done before. The saliva from our oral vessels served as a lip potion of sorts, covering the surface of my entire mouth. Greg held me firmly in his clutches, and softly asked, "Can you take the day off today, I'd like to spend the entire day with you making up for days wasted." "Yes, baby, I will take the day off for you. I will do anything for you. I love you, Baby," I said. There I was, unashamedly, standing there with an elevator filled with spectators witnessing our love and for once in a very long time allowing myself to let go, exhale and yes, be loved out loud. I was panting beyond control, and my dignity had been seared off like a useless skin tag. I was filled with complete excitement, and I loved every bit of it. Still wrapped in his arms, Greg with his deep masculine voice assured me that I meant the world to him, which left me euphoric. The titillating words that left his mouth, were warm and damp against my face. My adrenalin was off the Richter scale. Still in the elevator, I grew lightheaded from everything in that moment and could feel my body growing weaker and weaker under his spell. I ultimately collapsed into his arms, knowing he would be there to catch me.

"Ms. Ellison, are you ok? You fainted in the elevator. My name is Chessie, I am an EMT. Please remain calm, we are taking you to the E.R., here in Charlotte. Do you have a next of kin that we can call for you?" "What! The ER?" I screamed. "No, please don't call anyone. I am fine." I was still very lightheaded and was taken to the hospital where the medical staff ran a battery of tests and it was determined that I was severely hypoglycemic and dehydrated but otherwise ok, which accounted for why I fainted. I explained to the medical team that I had not eaten much over the past couple of days and would be fine. I was still in a fog and couldn't figure out where Greg had gone, because he was with me in the elevator, but I dare not elaborate too much about that, because nothing made sense. They provided me with a glass of orange juice and a peanut butter sandwich and released me, without incident.

In a panic I immediately contacted my job and informed them I had a family emergency, which prevented me from contacting them earlier. My manager was sympathetic and said she would cover my time away from the office with hours from my work compensation time balance. She further suggested that I take as much time as I needed to deal with my family emergency. I thanked my manager for her understanding and said I would continue to keep her posted. After speaking with my manager, I called a ride share service for a ride home. While in the vehicle, I began to reflect on the events of the day. I also began to read the ER discharge document and was embarrassed and shocked by how it read. Apparently, I had passed out in the elevator and was found by my neighbors on the elevator floor, alone, which is why an ambulance was called.

Needless to say, I never made it to Greg's unit, but I thought about him for the rest of the evening. I probably shouldn't make more of our situation-ship than it is. Yes, I let my guard down with him, but in all honesty, I don't regret it. I'm tired of making excuses for allowing myself to feel raw, organic emotions that align with who I am as a woman, a Nubian woman. I would faint in the elevator all over again, if it would prove to Greg how serious I am about our relationship.

It was about 10:30 p.m. when I received a notification that I had a text message. To my surprise it was Greg. I nearly dropped the phone when I saw his name scroll across my phone. I immediately clicked on his name, "My Boo" to read his message. Greg asked me how I was doing and went on to add that the door attendant at our condominium complex had informed him that I had a medical emergency while in the elevator and had to be taken to the hospital. Greg said he wanted to stop by to check on me but wasn't sure if I was still awake. I immediately called Greg and on the first ring he answered, "Hello sweetheart, how are you doing? Are you ok? I heard you had an incident in the elevator," he said. In my softest voice, I answered, "I'm doing ok, I just hadn't been eating properly and it caught up with me." "Would it be ok if I stopped by to check on you? I promise I won't be long, especially since it's a work night." I softly informed Greg that due to the earlier event in the elevator, I would be taking the rest of the week off and wouldn't be returning to work until the coming Monday. Before I could finish my sentence, Greg had made his way to my unit and was ringing my doorbell. I was still lying on my couch when he arrived. There I was, just me. No makeup, no perfume, and no idea what to expect from his visit.

I opened the door and Greg entered holding a grocery bag. "I come bearing gifts," he said with the most delicious smile on his face. Upon seeing this masterpiece of a man, somehow my energy returned. I was happy to see him and even happier that Greg was standing before me, because he wanted to be here, wanted to be near me. Greg walked over to the table and began to reveal the contents of the bag. "I hope you like spicy hummus! I also brought you organic grapes, baked thyme and garlic crackers and fresh garden salad. Did I do good?" He said. By now, I was staring at Greg, as if I were his wife. "You did good baby, but you always do good," I said. Greg blushed and walked over to me and took me by the hand and we both washed our hands in the kitchen sink. Greg took both of my hands and proceeded to assist me with washing my hands.

His technique for washing my hands was tender and just short of erotic. Greg used his thumbs to carefully clean the palms of my hands. When we finished washing our hands, we walked hand in hand over to the table and Greg proceeded to feed me slowly. No one had ever fed me, other than my mom, of course. "I know you want to know why you haven't heard from me, well, I'll tell you why," he said. "I realize we have spent some really special moments together, all of which means a lot to me. In fact, I have been thinking about our relationship and I didn't want to rush too quickly and thought it might be a good idea to pull back a little, but when I heard about the medical incident in the elevator, it made me realize how much you mean to me, and you need to know that." Greg said, in a very soft tone. I was sweating profusely and was looking into his eyes as he continued to explain himself. "Dakota," he said, "when you return to work on Monday, do you think you will be able to get an update on my business proposal and loan application? I know this isn't the best time to mention this, but I really need an update on where the bank is in the process, but of course your health and you feeling better is most important, right now". "Oh, sure, that won't be a problem at all. I'm feeling fine," I assured him. "Actually," I said softly, "I will send an email tomorrow to my colleague in charge of the review process and request an update." Greg leaned in and kissed me and then kissed me some more and more and then we woke up in each other's arms.

Somehow, being with him restored me. I felt like my old self again. Surprisingly, Greg took the day off from work and he and I spent the entire day talking and watching our favorite comedies. At one point I retreated to my laptop and pretended to send an email regarding the funding request for his proposal, but all I really did was send an email to myself with gibberish in the body of the email. When I returned to his arms, "Done!" I said assuredly. Greg kissed my forehead and whispered in my ear, "Thank you sweetheart." Greg left my condo around 7 p.m. He even texted me when he arrived at his unit, thanking me for a wonderful day, along with a heart emoji. I told him how much I enjoyed our time together and thanked him for dinner and so much more. I really love my Boo! During our time together, Greg said he would be busy over the next few days but would check in with me to make sure I'm ok. I slept extremely well that night and Greg even called me to make sure I was ok. He also insisted that I call him at any time of the day if I need to connect with him. This has been one the best days of my life.

# CHAPTER 10

It is now Monday morning and Greg and I have become extremely close and have spent every day together since the elevator incident.

My first day back at work was phenomenal. My colleagues were happy to see me and flooded my desk with flowers, along with a hot, delicious cup of lemon zinger tea, which is one of my absolute favorites. After exchanging niceties, I forewent my work breaks and pushed straight through the day. In doing so, I virtually eliminated or addressed every action item in my queue.

As I was leaving for the day, my manager, Marie Edgewater, stopped by to see if everything was ok with my family. On impulse,

I stated, "my family is doing great! Thank you for asking." I continued, "my parents are in the process of downsizing and looking forward to purchasing something a bit smaller and closer to the beach, so that my socialite mom and her friends can spend more time by the water. My mom is super psyched and has asked me to accompany her and my dad, next weekend to look at a few prospects." After I had assured her that my parents were fine, Marie, standing there a bit perplexed stated, "That's great, I'm happy to hear that everything is ok with your parents. I just assumed when you had the family emergency, it had something to do with your lovely parents." To run interference on the made-up family emergency scenario that permitted me to be away from work for several days, I immediately blurted out, "Yes, so, my grandparents were going through a very tough time medically. An emergency of sorts. Which is why I needed to be there to support my parents and grandparents, last week. However, things are much better now, and my grandparents are doing fine now." Marie had now adjusted her posture and was now standing directly in front of my desk with her arms folded tightly across her sternum. "I'm happy you were able to be there for your parents. That's what it's all about. Family. Right?" she said. Marie continued, "was it your mother's parents or your dad's parents?"

I had been an employee with my current employer for many years and during my tenure with the organization, both sets of my grandparents had long since passed and Marie had attended three of the four funerals. It immediately occurred to me that Marie knew I wasn't being truthful, so she stood there looking at me, motionless and speechless. To save face, I blurted out, "As you are aware, my grandparents are deceased, but the individual who experienced an emergency is an older aunt who was never married and has no children and due to her status, my family reveres her as a grandparent figure." Marie quietly muttered, "I see," as she locked eyes with me for a few seconds and without blinking, studied me for a few minutes, wished my family well and then exited my office. That whole encounter with my manager was super awkward and embarrassing to say the least. I respect Ms. Edgewater and have never lied to her about anything, until now.

While driving home from work that afternoon, it occurred to me that I hadn't seen my menstrual cycle. I've had problems with my menstrual in the past, so I'm sure it will show up eventually.

# CHAPTER 11

**A**fter the elevator incident, I realized I needed more time to recover from the fainting spell in the elevator. Apparently, when I fainted in the elevator, I hit the floor very hard, because my entire body, days later felt as if I had been hit by a freight train. In combing my hair, I discovered a large bump on the back of my head and observed a good amount of bruising to my entire back and elbow areas. My ankles were also a bit sore and swollen, which made it extremely uncomfortable to walk. In a panic, I contacted my job and requested three additional compensation days, to allow my body to heal. Ms. Edgewater was very understanding and sympathetic and advised me to take as much time as I needed. Ms. Edgewater suggested that I take the balance of the week off to address any personal issues and advised me to keep her updated accordingly. I said I would and ended the call.

I immediately called my mother to tell her how I was feeling but purposely failed to mention that I had fainted in the elevator the previous week. My mom insisted that I was coming down with the flu and wanted me to come home for a few days to rest up, which would also allow us to catch up. I agreed and told my mom I would be packing up a few items and would be on my way within the hour, especially since I knew it wasn't the flu.

I packed up a few things and called Greg to let him know that I was still feeling a bit under the weather and would be spending a few days at my parents' house, but he never answered the phone. I was feeling too unwell to process why he wasn't answering my calls and proceeded to make my way to my parents' home. My parents reside in a cozy suburb, located just outside of Charlotte, NC, and it's always a thrill to spend time at home with them, especially now, as I am not feeling particularly at my best.

When I arrived at my parent's house, I was actively throwing up and unable to physically stand on my own. Therefore, my dad had to assist me with exiting the vehicle and up to my room. My mother fixed me a cup of tea and a chick-pea salad rollup and then insisted that I take it easy for the rest of the day.

I spent the next few days in bed, hardly moving an inch. I don't even recall brushing my teeth, but what I do recall is Greg not returning any of my phone calls or responding to any of my text messages. I laid in bed thinking of reasons and excuses for why he was so on-and-off with me. On the fifth night, I felt much better and decided to go out for some fresh air. My parents had been a true blessing to me and nursed me back to health, albeit not completely though. Therefore, I decided to stay a few more days with them and then drive back home in the early part of the following week. That night, however, I decided to go for a drive to clear my head, in hopes of getting back to my old self again. My parents also thought it was a good idea for me to get out of bed and insisted I take a drive to get some fresh air. I agreed and grabbed a bottle of water and walked slowly to my vehicle. As I started to drive away from my parent's home, I began to reflect on the series of events that had transpired over the course of my life, especially in the past recent months, and began to weep. I tried to stay strong and reminded myself that being single is not the worst thing in life that can happen to me, but then the tears started even more, and I began recalling the many beautiful nights that Greg and I had spent together and then the next thing I knew, I was in the parking lot of my condominium complex. I don't even recall driving on the highway, everything was a blur. I sat in my car for a minute or two to collect myself, wipe away my tears and try to understand the reason for my premature return home. As I was gathering myself, through my blurred vision field I saw a vehicle pulling into the parking space perpendicular to my vehicle. The door opened and a very beautiful women emerged with a young child and they both entered the building. Seeing that beautiful family made me smile because the young boy was so adorable. I watched them enter the building and then realized how little sense it made for me to be sitting in a parking lot, instead of at my parents' home, resting. Thats when I decided to drive back to my parent's home, when suddenly, I spotted the young child and women emerge from the building, but his time the youngster was running top speed through the parking lot and dad was in hot pursuit behind him, especially since it was a very active parking lot. I lit up again to see what I wanted, a beautiful family of my own. Maybe a little one of my own. A husband. Someone to love. As the youngster bolted through the parking lot, I could see how frantic his dad was trying to catch him and wondered why mom was not as energetic, that's when it when I noticed the baby bump, which explained why she too, wasn't running behind the youngster. Apparently, the father caught up to the son, because I could hear him firmly addressing his son, "Little Man! Don't you ever do that again, do you hear me?" I wasn't trying to be nosey, but I could see through my blurry vision, what appeared to be the child's father, firmly picking up his son and walking him towards the child's mother. It was dusk by now, so I decided to head back to my parent's house. As I was leaving the parking lot, I could see the couple walking on the sidewalk area and the youngster was now in a stroller. It seemed as if they were out for a late afternoon, early evening walk. As I proceeded towards the exit area, I rolled down my window to bid them a good evening and that's when the couple turned and acknowledged my vehicle coming towards them and that was when I realized the gentleman was Greg. There he was, he had a whole family! I looked at him in disbelief, as he and his beautiful and very pregnant wife were walking right beside my vehicle. Greg looked at me as if I were a perfect stranger. His behavior was cold, distant, and mechanical. "Thank you, Ma'am," he said, as he pushed the stroller of his now sleeping baby onto the crosswalk that was in front of my vehicle. Everything in my mind went into slow motion, especially when I noticed the woman was wearing a wedding ring, which boasted at least 5 karats, at least that's how large the diamond appeared from my vantage point. As the pair walked through the crosswalk, Greg looked back to see if I was still watching him and his family and without any shame, he mouthed, "I'll call you later."

# CHAPTER 12

The drive back to my parent's house was beyond crazy. I must have pulled off the road a half dozen times, because I was crying so hysterically, I couldn't see in front of me. Lucky for me, when I arrived back at my parents' home, they had gone out for dinner and hadn't returned home yet. I made a mad dash to my room and called Greg no less than five hundred times, but he never answered. He later turned off his phone, so my calls went directly to his voicemail.

Now it all made sense. Greg is a married man. Where had his wife been the many nights Greg and I were together, from sunup to sundown? I had even checked the cabinets in his bathroom looking for confirmation of his status, but even that wasn't fool proof.

I spent two more days at my parent's house and then decided to head home. I wasn't feeling completely myself, but after Greg's betrayal, I don't think I will ever be.

When I arrived at my condominium building, I was filled with anxiety and prayed that I wouldn't run into Greg and his family again. I hurried into the elevator and thankfully, I was the only person on the elevator during my entire ascent to my unit. As I entered my unit, I noticed an envelope on the floor. Apparently, someone had slipped a notice of some kind under my door. The envelope was blank, but I could clearly see that there was a document inside. Since the envelope wasn't addressed to me, I assumed it was a notice from the condominium association, which usually arrives in the same fashion. Therefore, I flung the envelope in my stacked mail bin and proceeded to change my clothes and go for a short jog to clear my head. To my surprise I quickly completed the 5-mile run around the reservoir in record time and headed back home to watch one of my favorite programs. After returning home, I checked my text messages and incoming call log, but Greg had still not attempted to contact me.

I spent the balance of the week and weekend self-reflecting. To help with my blues, I reached out to several girlfriends, who I had met in college to catch up and to also take my mind off Greg. We had an awesome time and even discussed doing a *"girlfriend"* trip in the summer to Miami, which is one of my favorite cities to visit. It was also nice to hear them speak so lovingly about their significant other. We ended the lunch date on a high note, which left me feeling super hyped about myself and my personal future.

On my way home, I stopped to purchase some protein powder for my smoothie and a few items from the grocery store. When I emerged from the store, my nose encountered a scent that reminded me of Greg. I felt nostalgic for a minute, but quickly shrugged it off. I was trying to keep myself from tumbling into a deep depression since finding out Greg had a whole family and I had been his side chick. I was incensed, hurt, humiliated, and realized I couldn't even trust myself anymore when it came to men, because my judgment meter was completely damaged. I had been in several relationships and all of them ended nearly the same way, betrayal. But with Greg it was different. He was married with a family, perpetrating as a single man. We had been seeing each other a little more than three months and now this. Yes, he was sometimes hard to reach, but he always explained his disappearances and his justifications for disappearing at times, seemed to make sense. Greg is an aspiring businessperson, who is very much in the building phase of his career. Greg describes himself as a family-oriented person and I've often heard him speak highly of his parents and siblings. Greg presented strong, honest, and appeared to be very grounded as a beautiful Black man. And now this. I drove home quickly from the market and as I was exiting my vehicle, I saw Greg entering the building alone. I was so angry and excited all in that same moment, that I lost track of the intellectual element of my emotions. I waited in my vehicle for a bit, so that I wouldn't run into him in the lobby or elevator. After about 5 minutes or so, I decided to head for the elevator. As I entered the elevator, I could smell Greg's cologne still permeating every air pocket of the enclosure. The oxygen in the elevator smelled delicious, strong, and warm, just like Greg. On the ride up in the elevator, I closed my eyes and on purpose inhaled and exhaled at least one hundred times to savor every ounce of his masculine, delicious scent into my being.

When the elevator signaled for my floor, I quickly opened my eyes and there he was, standing at the elevator entrance waiting for me. "How are you doing," Greg said. His voice was soft with an apologetic tone. In shock and still hurt from his betrayal, I brushed past him and hurried to my condo unit. Greg trailed behind me insisting that he needed to talk with me and could explain everything. I stopped at my door and turned towards him to address him, but in that moment, I could feel my eyes beginning to fill with water and that's when he came closer to me and kissed me on the cheek and with a soft tone in my ear, he whispered, "I'm sorry for any pain that I have caused you, sweetheart, but I can explain everything. Please let me come in. I miss you and need for you to understand what's going on with me."

# CHAPTER 13

Greg's presence had always left me completely transfixed, which is why it was hard to pull away from his much-wanted affection, even though I was terribly upset with him. I wrapped my arms around his neck and began to weep. In that moment I was powerless, weak, and vulnerable. I wanted all of what I saw to be a dream. Just then, Greg whispered, "It's not what you think." Pulling away and looking in his beautiful face, I asked, "Then what is it? Who is that woman I saw you with and is that your child?" "Yes, that is my child and no it's not my girlfriend. We used to date. It was a very open, *on-and-off* relationship and that's when she became pregnant with my second child."

He continued, "Dakota, baby, I didn't know how to tell you about my situation, which is why I am truly sorry you had to find out this way." I hugged him tighter and looked into his eyes and said, "Are you sure she's not your wife and you're not married?" In the most assuring voice ever, he stated, "I am positively sure, that I am not married. My situation is complicated, but I am not married and need you to believe that." I continued, "Then why was she wearing a set of wedding rings?" Greg assured me that the two of them were once engaged, but never married and once the relationship ended, she wouldn't return the rings and continued to wear them. He continued, "We have not been in a committed relationship in three to four months, which is right around the time you and I started spending time together. Dakota, you never asked about my relationship status or my past, which is why I never discussed it." I pressed myself closer to him and kissed his soft, beautiful mouth and said, "you're right, I never asked." We hugged each other tightly for what seemed like forever. Neither of us said a word, we were there locked into each other, bonding more than we'd ever had.

I was super relieved that Greg wasn't married. However, I still had more questions but didn't want to ruin the moment by continuing to question him. Greg went on to express his genuine interest in me and stated that he was relieved that I now knew about the complicated situation with his ex. I told Greg that I was happy he'd come clean with me regarding his situation and assured him that I understood his hesitancy to share more about that part of his life.

We spent the balance of the evening making up for lost time, but this time it was different. Greg was even more affectionate than before. He spent most of our time together holding me and planting soft kisses on my face and forehead, which is how I fell asleep, in his arms and close to his heart. It was special.

Greg left my condo about 7:00 a.m. and asked if he could take me to dinner, around 5:30 p.m.

I immediately agreed and said I would call him later. I spent most of the day reflecting on my night with Greg and his account of his relationship with his ex. I ended my work 30 minutes earlier than usual, so that I would have ample time to arrive home to freshen up for my dinner date with my boo. Since Greg was going to be coming from an appointment, he texted me earlier in the day and told me where to meet him for dinner. Greg had planned a very romantic dinner at one my favorite restaurants, in the downtown district of Charlotte, where they have a whole menu of vegan entrees.

Since we were starting fresh, I wanted to wear something special. Therefore, I wore a flirty, teal colored, knee length dress with matching strappy sandals and adorned my entire body in my favorite body butter. Since Greg would be driving from one of his appointments, I decided not to drive my own vehicle and instead called for a rideshare service to pick me up and drop me at the restaurant.

Greg had made reservations for 5:30 p.m., so when I arrived at 5:20 p.m., I entered the restaurant, gave Greg's name to the waitstaff, and was escorted to my table, which was perfectly situated under soft lights with a candle strategically placed in the center of the table.

I had been waiting at the restaurant for thirty minutes when I received a text from Greg, stating that he had just arrived and was handing his vehicle over to the valet. It didn't matter to me that he was late arriving for our date. Greg was a hardworking businessman and, besides, we were starting a new chapter and I refused to give myself permission to be upset by his tardiness. He was all mine and that is all that mattered. When Greg entered the restaurant, it was as if time stood still, and everything was in slow motion. I was breathless watching my chocolate stallion walking towards me, yes, ME, Dakota! No man had ever made me feel this important, or wanted, or crazy in love. As Greg approached the table, he leaned into me for a tender peck, but not before whispering, "Dakota, you look beautiful tonight. I've been thinking about us all day." On impulse, Greg held my face and we kissed passionately before he seated himself across from me.

Greg's kisses always taste and smell like him, but this time his kisses were different and had an odor that could be misinterpreted in the worst of ways. "How was your day, sweetheart," I asked. "My day was great, but it's better now that I'm here with you," he said. I giggled, but I was still focusing on the taste and smell of Greg's kiss. During dinner, we had dinner, held hands, and agreed we would be completely exclusive, which is all I ever wanted.

When we arrived back to my condo, Greg excused

himself to shower and freshen up and I helped myself to the pockets of his jacket and slacks, hoping to make some sense of the unpleasant smell that had hijacked Greg's oral cavity and his beautiful lips. When Greg returned from showering and brushing his teeth, I had quickly finished riffling through his pocket and had now positioned myself at the foot of the bed, forcing a fake smile. As he approached me, he kissed me on my mouth and said, "Ok, Bae, it's your turn." I smiled and headed towards the shower, but still distracted by the smell that had now somehow vanished. That night we just held each other and drifted off to sleep, which was a first.

# CHAPTER 14

The smell on Greg's breath haunted me for weeks, because it felt like he had been with someone intimately prior to our dinner date and the odor that I encountered from kissing him was not in any way food related. I stifled my feelings on the matter and proceeded to love Greg with every ounce of my being. Our relationship was going well, and I did not want anything to rock our relationship.

Greg is very busy with work, but he and I manage to see each other at least three to four times a week. Greg never talks about his ex, and I am careful not to ask any questions. Greg told me that he wanted to introduce me to his son, but he was waiting for the right time to do so. Interestingly, he never mentioned the unborn child that his ex-girlfriend is carrying, or the impending due date of his second child. I am a bit nervous that things will change between Greg and I once his second child is born and I honestly can't bear the thought of it.

I am not sure how I feel about being a stepmother, because I promised myself, I would never date a man with children. I honestly know myself; I can't compete with the whole other family thing, and I am not sure if I want to take care of someone else's children, who may not even like me. I also don't want to be a built-in babysitter, as a byproduct of falling in love with a "baby daddy".

When I fell madly in love with Greg, I did not sign up for stepparenting, and I didn't sign up for babysitting. I signed up to only love him. I feel like I am forever making sacrifices and I am afraid as much as I love Greg, this sacrifice is beyond my reach. I will not tell him that of course, but I will make sure I pretend to be excited to meet his son but will make sure it never happens. I will always conveniently and convincingly find a reason to not be available.

# CHAPTER 15

Things have slowed down a bit at the office, so the vibe is super chill at work. I decided I would use this slow period at work to clean my office and catch up on my filing. While filing, I ran across Greg's business proposal and loan application that I had never submitted. It was crumpled and soiled with food stains, so I panicked and shredded it.

I wrapped up early at the office and decided to head home to prepare for an early run around the reservoir. I arrived home with ample time to chat with my mom, grab a quick snack and head out for a much-needed run. I returned home from my run feeling super upbeat and headed to the shower. While in the shower I could hear my phone ringing repeatedly from my bedroom. Drenched and only half showered, I made a mad dash to the phone, but the phone stopped ringing. I returned to the bathroom, finished showering, wrapped myself in my favorite robe and proceeded to read my notifications. I saw three incoming missed calls from Greg, but no message. Before I could return Greg's call, my phone rang again, and it was Greg. I immediately answered, "Hey Sweetie, are you ok?" I uttered in my sweetest voice. Greg's silence was concerning. "Yes, everything is fine. I, I, I just need to talk with you. Julia, my ex, delivered the baby last night… She and the baby are fine, but I really need to talk with you," Greg said, in an incredibly sad tone. "Of course, honey. I'm here for you. Are you at the hospital," I said in a very concerned voice. Fighting back tears, Greg told me that his ex-fiancé called him when she was enroute to the hospital at around 9:30 p.m., the previous night and when he arrived at the hospital she was in active labor and fully dilated. Greg went on to say that he was present for the birth of the child, but when the child was born the child had blond hair and green eyes. According to Greg, he lost his composure in the delivery room and was thrown out of the room and asked not to return until he had calmed down. Greg stated that at 11:30 p.m., he went home to cool off and returned to the hospital today around noon to find his ex-fiancé Julia, the baby, Julia's parents, and a male of Caucasian persuasion beaming and taking pics with the baby. Greg said Julia asked him to leave, because he was not the father of her newborn, as Jeff, the Caucasian gentleman that was there in the room was the father. Greg said he was devastated but left quietly and drove around for hours before going to work and calling me. In a very broken tone, Greg said he didn't want to go home, so I met him at his office and from there we just sat in his car where we were able to talk freely. During our time in the vehicle, Greg received several text messages and after collecting himself, he decided to look at his messages. After reading the messages, Greg handed me his phone and exited his vehicle and began quietly sobbing outside of the car. "What is it, Sweetie?" I asked gently. I continued, "What happened? As I looked down at his phone, I saw four messages from Julia stating that they were on a break when she conceived, so it should not come as a complete surprise to him that she was involved with other people, while still dealing with him. To add insult to injury, Julia went on to add that the child that he believed to be his, may not be his and she was asking him to pay for a paternity test to determine the paternity of their toddler, either way. Julia ended the text with, "I didn't mean to hurt you, but you and I have never been faithful to one another, so you shouldn't be completely surprised by this news. Let me know about the paternity test idea, I want closure. BTW, our hookups end today."

After reading the text, I climbed out of the car to console Greg, but not before sending that text message to myself and deleting any evidence of my actions from Greg's phone. Greg was devastated, because he never said another word for the rest of the evening and on the drive home, I held his strong hand and counted the sweet tears that cascaded down his beautifully melanated skin, on to his light gray, cotton, button down, starched shirt. Greg dropped me off at our condominium complex and said he needed to be alone. I told him I understood and to call me if he needed me. I held him, kissed his strong forehead, and exited the vehicle.

When I entered the building and was alone in the elevator, I could barely contain myself. I needed to read that text message again, especially the part about the "BTW our hookups end today." That explains that funny smell on his face and on his stinky breath during our dinner date last month. That might also explain why we just cuddled that night. That might explain a lot of things.

# Chapter 16

It's Friday evening and the week has been an emotional rollercoaster, especially for Greg. He invited me to join him at his parent's house this evening for a small gathering, sort of a family, fun night. The festivities are scheduled to start at 7:30 p.m. I guess it's their way of cheering him up and taking his mind off the latest developments. This will be my first time meeting his parents and family. I've spoken to them on the phone through Greg, but never in person. Therefore, tonight will be special. Greg is finally including me in his life in a major way and even though I have many questions for him regarding his Ex's text message, specifically about the "hooking up," comment, I still feel it's a step in the right direction. I guess I have his ex-fiancé to thank, because her ambiguity regarding the paternity of his children has strengthened our beautiful relationship, in a very short span of time.

Greg's parents live in an upscale, pristine community, North of Charlotte, NC. To avoid the weekend traffic, Greg and I agreed to leave early so that we would arrive on time. The energy in the car was thick during our drive to Greg's Parent's home. Therefore, I purposely paired my phone with the Bluetooth in Greg's vehicle and played my favorite, most relaxing jazz music.

As we were driving, Greg took my hand and began

sobbing uncontrollably. He pulled over onto the shoulder of the Expressway and began confessing his love for me and telling me how sorry he was for hurting me. Greg admitted he had been hooking up with his ex while dating me, but said the whole ordeal was just a "*thing*" and didn't mean anything to him. Greg went on to profess his love for me and wanted nothing more than to marry me in the future and start a family. I was shocked by his confession and emotional state, but happy to know how much he loved and cared for me. I told Greg I wanted the same thing, even though having children is not part of my future plans, I think. Ok, so I lied to him because that's what he deserved, especially since he betrayed me. Nonetheless, we kissed, but not before I slapped his cheating, lying face for exposing me to his dirty, nasty habits and then held him as tightly as possible, assuring him that no matter what, I would be there for him, but warned him I would be gone in a heartbeat if he ever disrespected me again. Having that exchange with Greg was necessary because we needed to clear the air prior to arriving at his parents' house.

Ok, the part about him pulling over and professing his love for me and the slap, never happened. In fact, all of that was wishful thinking on my part. What really happened was, during the entire commute to his parents' home, we barely held hands, it was as if I were invisible. Had it not been for the playlist that was playing, the silence in the vehicle would have been even more uncomfortable than knowing Greg had been purposely playing me. To be perfectly honest, once we started our commute, Greg appeared to be in another world and barely glanced in my direction, except for that one time when I paired my phone with his blue tooth in his vehicle. That's it.

When we arrived at Greg's parent's home, there were several people on the porch and as we pulled into the driveway and exited the vehicle, Greg's mom made her way to the vehicle and began hugging Greg, a hug that a loving mom gives to her son who is deeply hurting. After about a minute or so, Greg introduced me to his beautiful mother and we both embraced and headed into the house. Greg's mom looked to be in her late sixties, slender stature, extremely attractive and well put together.

The night was amazing. There were about fifty guests, which consisted of family and friends. The atmosphere was filled with laughter and great conversation and Greg's paternity dilemma never surfaced in any of the many conversations. Greg's mom was pleasant, but in an eerie way. I caught Greg's mom staring at me on many occasions, but I chalked it up to her trying to get to know me, her future daughter in-law.

However, on the way to the restroom I overheard her telling her husband that I didn't look like Greg's type, and she didn't think our relationship was serious. She then chuckled and blurted out, "she'll be another statistic once the financing is approved for his business. That's the only reason he still has her hanging around." Greg's mom went on to add, "I'm sure she knows she's not the only one. Greg is still very committed to his bachelor life, and I hope he is not leading this young lady on." Hearing Greg's mom's sentiments was a huge setback for me. When I returned from the restroom, I seated myself quietly away from the festivities and occupied myself on my cell phone. Several people came over to check on me, but I assured them that I was fine and then pretended to be responding to work related matters on my phone, when in fact I was taking pictures of Greg's parents' home and others at the party, but mostly Greg.

The festivities wrapped up around 11:30 p.m. and by then I was beyond ready to go home and unpack the events of the day. Greg's parents waved goodbye from the porch, and we were on our way. The drive home was worse than the drive there. I was hurt by Greg's mom's comments but knew the ride home was not the best time to bring it up. Greg was already dealing with disappointing news from earlier in the day, so I decided to just remain calm and stuff it down, just like I do everything else.

During the ninety-minute drive back home, I guess Greg noticed my energy had shifted and asked if I was ok. I flashed a fake smile and told him I was fine and assured him I was tired from the exceptionally long day. That was the only verbal exchange between the two of us for the entire commute back home. Once we arrived at the parking lot, Greg parked his vehicle and we both exited the vehicle and began walking towards the building. Greg saw me to my condo, gave me a quick peck on the lips and mouthed the words, "I'll try to call you later." I flashed another perfectly fake smile and said, "Ok" and quickly entered my unit, but not before noticing that Greg had an incoming call that he casually answered as he was walking towards the elevator. I'm sure it wasn't his mom checking to see if he had arrived home safely and it certainly wasn't me. Feeling vulnerable at that moment, I involuntarily blurted out, "Good night baby, I love you", but Greg kept walking and never turned around to acknowledge my profession of love. Well, to be perfectly honest, I didn't actually annunciate my love for him out loud at that moment, it was all in my head.

# CHAPTER 17

It was now 3:07 a.m., and there I was lying flat on my back in bed staring at the glare from the streetlights that cozily illuminated my bedroom. At least one million and one thoughts about Greg's deception and his mom's feelings towards me raced through my head. I had images of Greg spending intimate moments with his ex and then intentionally exposing me to the nastiness of it all. Not to mention, had his ex-fiancé Julia not put an end to their "hook up sessions" that whole charade would still be in full swing, unbeknownst to me. Yes, there were red flags when I saw the two of them together in the parking lot, but Greg explained everything to me, and I felt I could trust his account of their relationship. And now it feels like I am back to square one.

I feel like such an idiot and now, Greg expects me to coddle him through his latest bout of disappointments. I am so angry with him for implying to his mom that I am only around to assist him with securing financing for his impending business venture. Little does he know; I have shredded his proposal and will continue to string him along until he's tired of being dragged. My mind begs the question, who could have been calling him at 2:00 a.m.? My head is pounding, thinking of how I am being played.

It is now 6:00 a.m. and I'm still awake, still thinking of

ways to learn more about Greg, and who he really is. To relax my mind, I decided to go for an early Saturday morning run, which always helps to calm and relax me. I dressed quickly and was on my way. As I exited the building, I couldn't help but notice that Greg's vehicle was not in the parking spot he had parked in when he and I arrived at the complex around 1:00 a.m., earlier that morning. Curious, I pretended to do a warmup jog around the parking lot, looking to see if Greg had moved his vehicle, but to my disappointment, Greg's car was nowhere to be found. I eventually exited the parking lot to start my run. I ran for approximately 90 minutes, arriving back to the condominium complex around 8:00 a.m.

After a long hot shower, and with my mind now clear, I decided to give Greg some space and not deal with his shenanigans and lying ways. To take my mind off my situation, I decided to reach out to my besties, and we all met for lunch and an early movie. I didn't mention anything about Greg, because I didn't want the Greg thing to overshadow the great time we were having. After a fun time with the girls, I ran a few errands and decided to head home.

When I pulled in the lot, Greg's vehicle was now in his usual parking spot. As I entered the elevator for some reason, I felt a pull to visit Greg, even though I had determined earlier to distance myself from him, but I needed to see him and to learn of his whereabouts when he left my unit. Therefore, I exited the elevator at Greg's floor, walked to his unit and rang the bell. I waited for about a minute and rang the bell again. After about 3 minutes more, Greg opened the door and was surprised to see me standing there. "Hello, Greg, I was stopping by to see how you are doing and if you need anything," I said. It was clear that Greg had someone in his unit because he just stood there in the doorway, in his robe, with little to say. Finally, Greg, in a soft quiet voice said, "I'm fine, I am tired from the long drive last night, coupled with everything else I'm going through right now. In fact, I haven't left my bed since I walked you up to your unit early this morning." Totally disgusted by his blatant lie, I said "Oh, my, I can only imagine what you must be going through." I asked Greg if I could use his restroom, but he dodged the question and said he wanted to go back to bed and thanked me for understanding. Greg said he would call me later and closed the door right in my face.

Embarrassed and mortified, I returned to my condo fuming mad, and certain that what I overheard Greg's mom saying about Greg and my relationship was completely true. Greg didn't want me, nor did he respect me and now I was on a mission to find out his true motive even if it was on my last breath.

I grabbed my car keys and returned to the lot; I was determined to find out who was in Greg's unit. I carefully parked my vehicle in clear view of Greg's vehicle and positioned myself in my vehicle in an inconspicuous manner, incognito style. I watched Greg's vehicle for hours, hoping he would surface with his mysterious companion, but to no avail. My legs had grown numb from being seated in a contorted manner and I was about to abandon my mission, when Greg and a male companion emerged from the building together, laughing and walking towards a vehicle in the distance that I had not seen before. I felt a sense of relief, when I saw that he had been hanging out with one of his buddies and not a woman. In fact, I felt convicted by my jealousy and felt sincere remorse for my sinister behavior. I continued to watch my man from the distance. I watched Greg and his friend chat for a bit, give a quick fist bump and then the visitor entered his vehicle, rolled down the driver's side window and that's when Greg leaned in and gave his male visitor a passionate kiss before walking quickly back towards the building.

I could hardly believe my eyes and was in utter shock. Greg's visitor was now leaving the lot and my instinct was to know more about the gentleman and what I had just seen. I started my car and began following the vehicle to get a closer look at the person in question. I managed to catch up to the vehicle and followed the car to a nearby strip mall. The gentleman parked his vehicle and that's when I also parked in an adjacent parking spot and managed to position myself directly behind the incredibly attractive male, who entered an upscale unisex hair salon. I was determined to get a closer look at Greg's suitor and after about five minutes I entered the salon pretending to need hair service. The interior design of the shop was on trend and the décor was exquisite. The lighting was warm, the music was on point and there were patrons seated in the posh waiting area. It was as if everything were an illusion because time started to speed up and I could hardly catch my breath. Then out of nowhere, I heard a strong masculine voice say, "Good afternoon, my name is Yriah, would you like assistance with signing in?" There were a dizzying number of mirrors everywhere, and I wasn't sure where the voice resonated from, until I took a cleansing breath and looked directly in the face of Greg's suiter who was standing just to my left flashing the most handsome smile I had ever seen. After staring at him for about fifteen seconds, studying his jawline and recalling his romantic interaction with Greg, I replied, "Yes, that would be nice." Yriah, continued, "Are you a first-time customer? I don't recall ever seeing you in the salon." My response was immediate, "Yes, this is my first time visiting. I've heard so much about the salon and since I was in the area today, I decided to stop in to check it out", I fibbed, nervously. Yriah proceeded to walk me over to the sign-in kiosk and asked me for my name. I told him my name was Sky and he began filling out the electronic intake form, based on the information that I provided to him. I thanked Yriah for his assistance and assured him that I was comfortable with navigating the intake form, but not before he slipped me his business card, which clearly identified him as the owner of the salon. Once again, I thanked

Yriah for sharing his business contact information with me and for assisting me with the sign-in process. The salon offered many services, so I opted for the eyebrow maintenance service. I was advised the wait would be ninety minutes and at a cost of one hundred fifty dollars, which is expensive by any standard.

After registering, I found a cozy spot in the waiting area and decided to spend my wait time of ninety minutes, actively looking up the owner of the shop, Yriah Smalls. After perusing the internet for about fifteen minutes I was able to discern that Yriah Smalls lived in an upscale community in a beautiful new construction, with his wife and three children.

Yriah was a Morehouse Alumnus and a philanthropist. I could not believe what I was reading and began second guessing the fact that I saw Greg making out with Yriah, a married pillar in the community.

In the distance I could hear the receptionist call out, "Sky, Ms. Sky, we're ready for you." I didn't see anyone walking in her direction, so I decided to continue with my research, until a perfect pair of pumps appeared directly in front of me, which forced me to look up to see the receptionist standing before me, "Ms., is your name Sky?" she said. This time her question was more direct and filled with curiosity. "Yes, yes! I am so sorry. Please forgive me, that's what happens when you're addicted to online shopping," I said. We both laughed and I followed her to one of the suites to meet the technician who would be performing the service.

The eyebrow technician identified herself, but I couldn't recall her name. The process was so relaxing that I fell asleep as soon as I hit the chair. I had been awake for more than twenty-four hours, so I was exhausted. After around forty minutes, I was awakened by the technician and asked to pay on the way out. I did manage to get a glimpse in the mirror at my brows and to my surprise, I loved my fresh look. The technician had shaped my eyebrows in accordance with the shape of my face, which really freshened up my look. I paid on the way out, but not before looking back to say goodbye to Yriah.

# CHAPTER 18

When I arrived home, I was drained and really couldn't give the whole mess with Greg any more brain energy. Therefore, I got a quick snack and crashed on my couch. I woke up Sunday morning at 4:00 a.m., the next day. I felt refreshed, but troubled and a bit anxious. I thought about Greg's double life and how he has been deceiving his parents, lying to me, and living recklessly. In my mind I began to ponder exactly how many more people Greg was intimately involved with, because in less than twenty-four hours, I learned that Greg had been romantically involved with at least two other people while dealing with me. Without question, Greg has proven to be an intentional heart-slaying predator, who is on a mission to destroy every heart in his path. I am feeling terrified, because I have been feeling a bit off for a few months now but didn't think it was anything serious, but with the latest development concerning Greg's serial promiscuity and my irresponsibility, first thing tomorrow morning, before work, I will visit the walk-in clinic and request an STD screening and pray for the best.

I spent my entire Sunday resting in bed, watching my favorite comedies, and nibbling on celery and humus. Greg never called, but did send a text at 8:00 p.m., asking if I could give him an update on the status of his business loan application. He said he needed an update for an important upcoming meeting with a potential funder on Tuesday. I told him I would check the status and provide him with an update in the morning, which couldn't have been furthest from the truth, on my part.

The rest of the night dragged on, and it took every ounce of restraint in my being for me to not visit Greg's condo to confront him about his lies and double life, but I knew it would get messy and not end well. I was extremely emotional and went through a myriad of emotions, ranging from rage to deeply missing Greg. I was a wreck but managed to contain myself and eventually nodded off.

I awoke early on Monday morning and made my way to the walk-in clinic. I was given a pelvic exam and sent to the lab to have my blood screened and then immediately headed to work. My workday started out great. I arrived around 8 a.m. and worked nonstop until my manager walked into my office around 1:00 p.m. and stated that she had been contacted by Mr. Gregory Wayland requesting an update on his small business financing application with the bank. She went on to say that the documents were hand delivered to me approximately five months ago and I had informed Mr. Wayland that the documents were in process. My initial response was to lie about having any knowledge of the paperwork or Greg, but she could tell I was scrambling in my words and before I could answer, she asked that I prepare for an impromptu meeting in the conference room in fifteen minutes and to bring the initial application and supporting documentation. When I arrived at the conference room, I was empty handed. On one side of the conference table, Greg was seated next to the VP of financing for the bank, and I sat next to my manager on the opposite side of the table. I was now facing Greg and knew the meeting would not end well for me. Greg began explaining that my inaction caused him an important business deal and he demanded that the bank handle the matter and expedite the processing of his application, immediately.

Embarrassed and humiliated by Greg's appearance at my place of employment, I remained silent and calmly stated that I did not recall receiving anything from the gentleman and reminded the group that I am not responsible for reviewing business plans, or processing business loan applications, which may account for the mix up. Greg became irate and began accusing me of sabotaging him and threatened to sue the bank. Sensing things were getting out of control, my manager asked me to excuse myself from the meeting and approximately twenty minutes after returning to my office, my manager visited my office again, but this time to inform me that I needed to take the rest of the day off. I gathered my things and headed to my vehicle. I was defenseless and knew my job was now seriously in jeopardy. When I reached my vehicle, Greg was calling me on my cell phone, or so I thought, because upon closer inspection I realized it was the clinic calling with a message for me to call back immediately. I hurriedly called back the clinic and requested to speak to the nurse. I was placed on hold, and after a 2 minute wait the nurse picked up the phone and stated that my results from the lab were complete and I needed to visit the clinic to review the results. I begged the nurse to please share the results with me on the phone, but she, in a calm voice said, "Ms. Ellison, I think it's best if you come in to go over your results and you may want to bring someone with you." I began sobbing uncontrollably. The nurse then suggested that I not drive in my current state and consider calling a rideshare service. I assured her I was ok and was on my way. The nurse said, "Ok, dear. Please be careful and proceed directly to adult internal medicine when you arrive. I'll be waiting for you there" and then ended the call.

I was glazed over during the entire commute to the clinic. I had a massive headache and could hardly breathe. When I arrived at the walk-in clinic, in my haste, I double parked in front of the building, dashed inside, and sprinted to my Dr.'s office. As I entered the office, I identified myself and was met by the nurse and was escorted to a small private office. Before I could ask any questions, the nurse began reading the report, and started the conversation with, "Well, Ms. Ellison, I will get to the point, but you have a lot to process right now." "What do you mean by that" I said. The nurse continued, "You are about eight weeks pregnant, and you are also HIV positive." At which time she handed me the report from the lab. The nurse went on to ask, "Are you currently in a relationship? Due to your status, your partner will need to be notified and anyone else you may have been sexually involved with." The nurse advised me that I would need to seek medical follow up immediately and scheduled my appointment for the next day.

I left the clinic weighed down from the events of the day, only to find my vehicle on the back of a flatbed, soon to be hauled away. The tow truck driver had secured the vehicle on the back of his truck and advised me that the only way to get around the physical tow is to pay him in full to drop the vehicle. Otherwise, I would have to follow him to the tow yard which was six miles away. I was too weak to fight with him, so I paid him two-hundred dollars and he backed my vehicle off the flatbed. I needed a good cry and burst into tears as soon as I was safely seated in my vehicle. My head was still throbbing, but I made it home safely. I collapsed on the sofa and prayed that the day was just a dream, until I received a call from my manager. I was a total wreck and refused to pick up. Therefore, she left a voicemail message advising me to check my email. Upon checking my email, I intercepted a communication from my manager informing me that I was being placed under suspension, until an investigation regarding the mishandling of Greg's documents was complete.

# CHAPTER 19

My world was spinning out of control, and I did not have anyone that I could trust with my latest developments, except Greg. I have loving parents who love me and would be devastated to learn that in one day I have been suspended from my job, have contracted HIV and pregnant. In a panic, I reached out to Greg, but he had blocked my number. I let out a scream that I am sure the whole building heard, but no one came. I called my manager, but my call went to her voicemail. I left a message pleading with her to call me. I wanted to call my besties, but I knew this was more than any of them could handle, so I sat on the floor in my bedroom and prayed that it was all a figment of my imagination, just like before, but it wasn't. It was my reality. I cried myself to sleep on the floor. When I awoke it was 8:57 p.m. and I felt desperately alone.

I tried calling Greg again, but my number was still blocked and that is when my anxiety turned to anger and then rage. How dare he turn my world upside down and then block my calls. Many things went through my mind concerning Greg and none of them were rational. Greg needed to explain why he deliberately infected me with HIV. Greg also needed to pay for his part in my suspension from my place of employment, where I had earned respect from my peers and had maintained a perfect attendance record, until I met him. Greg also needs to know that I am carrying his child.

I decided to pay Greg a visit to have him explain why he upended my life. When I arrived at his condo, I rang the bell and could hear a lot of movements on the other side of the door, as if someone were moving furniture, or dragging something. "Open the door, Greg! I hear you moving around! If you do not open the door, I will kick it in!" I yelled in my loudest voice ever, but the movements behind the door continued, and he never opened the door. I began banging on his door with my fist and proceeded to kick the door with my foot, but the only doors opening were the doors of the other residents. "Ms. Ellison are you ok?" one person asked. Another person warned me that if I continued kicking the door and disturbing the peace, they would call the police. I heeded the warning, ended my mission, and headed back to my condo unit to initiate plan B, which was to find his vehicle and damage it to the fullest. I was sure I would hear from him then.

I returned to my condo and grabbed a can of red spray paint, a box cutter, hammer, fingernail polish remover and any other tool I needed to make my point and get Greg's attention. I was spinning out of control, but nothing mattered and plus, my love for Greg had now turned to pure hate. I placed the objects in my backpack and headed down to the parking lot to exact my revenge on his vehicle, but not before I sent him a text message stating, "You'll pay for what you've done to me, and you'll be sorry you blocked my number!" I made my way to the parking lot, where I spotted Greg's car parked in an unusual spot, as if he were trying to hide it from me. I removed the spray paint from my bag and began spraying the vehicle. I slashed all four of his tires and sprayed the following words on the hood of his metallic cream Lexus 460 GX, "I HATE YOU!", not before spitting on his vehicle. Someone spotted me in the parking lot vandalizing Greg's vehicle and yelled, "Stop, I'm calling the police." I secured the spray paint can in my backpack, left the parking lot area and returned to Greg's condo. Upon my arrival, I began knocking on the door when I noticed the door was partially open. I pushed the door open and began screaming "Greg, Greg, where are you?" As I walked towards his bedroom the lights were out and through the shadows, I saw him asleep on the bed. I ran over to him and started pummeling him and screaming, "Get up! I hate you!" Right around that time I realized he was not responding, which is when I heard footsteps entering the room followed by a beam of light that illuminated my face and overtook my vision. "This is the Charlotte police, put your hands up and lower yourself to the floor." The officer commanded. And within a millisecond, the bedroom lights came on and I saw Greg lying in a pool of blood barely breathing. There was blood all over the bed, the floor and now all over me! "What happened to him? I didn't do anything?" I said, in a bone curdling scream. With their weapons still trained on me, I was grabbed, thrown into the wall and handcuffed.

As I was escorted out of Greg's unit, I could see trails of blood throughout the living room area. I looked at the officer and continued to proclaim my innocence. I was paraded through the lobby where my fellow tenants watched me being led away in handcuffs, away from what was an obvious crime scene. They read me my Miranda Rights and the only part that echoed in my head was, "You have the right to remain silent. Anything you say can and will be held against you in a court of law…." I kept asking the officers if Greg was ok, but they wouldn't answer. As I was being processed from the back of the police vehicle, I could see swarms of ambulances rushing into the parking lot and running into the building with a stretcher and other equipment. The flashing red lights from the emergency vehicles were blinding, and it all seemed like a scene from a horrible movie, except it wasn't.

When we arrived at the police station, I was processed,

fingerprinted, and taken to a room, where I was advised I could make one phone call before being taken to my cell. I said I wanted to call my parents. It was 11:11 p.m. and my mom picked up the phone on the first ring. "Dakota, honey, are you ok?" Mom said excitedly. "I heard there was an incident at your complex, are you ok?" Sobbing uncontrollably, I answered, "No, mom, I am not ok. I have been locked up. I can explain everything, but can you and dad come down here, PLEASE?" The officer removed the phone from my hand and told my parents which precinct I was being held in and then ended the call. I was taken to my cell and stayed there until my parents arrived the next day with our family attorney. As I sat across from my parents and was not permitted to embrace them. I was advised to keep my hand on the table, which is when I saw mom's tear-filled eyes staring at the red stains all over my hands and nailbeds. My mom began to sob uncontrollably, and my dad pulled her into his massive chest, and fought back his own tears as he determined to stay strong. My parents were speechless and the way they looked at me broke my heart. They were disappointed, but most of all confused.

Mr. Reynolds, the family attorney leaned across the table towards me and said, "Dakota, you are facing several serious charges and I will do everything legally possible to help you, but

I will need to know everything that transpired, leading up to you being found in the victim's bedroom covered in blood and a backpack filled with weapons and other objects. I need the complete truth. Do you understand?" I nodded my head in acknowledgement and said I could explain everything. To which Mr. Reynolds replied, "Can you?" He went on to say that my bail was set at five hundred thousand dollars, and he would do everything legally possible to have that figure reduced.

My parents were asked to leave the room and that's when Attorney Reynolds' assistant entered the room and positioned herself directly in front of me and said, "I need you to start from the very beginning. When did you first meet the victim, Mr. Gregory Wayland and do you have a reason to want to see him harmed in any way?" I placed my stained hands on my pitiful head and reluctantly said, "Yes, but I swear to you I am not the one who hurt him." There was a deafening silence in the room, perhaps one of disbelief and after about thirty seconds, Attorney Reynolds announced that he and his assistant would be leaving to address any new updates concerning my bail but would be returning later to pick up where we left off.

As my attorney exited the room, a very tall female officer entered the room and asked me to stand to my feet. I was then cuffed and led back to my cell via a corridor where my dear, and loving parent's eyes locked with mine in the distance, as I was led away in shame, sorrow and in shackles.

# Chapter 20

The walk back to my cell was traumatic and lonely, but mostly confusing. To make matters worse, in the distance I could hear my mother sobbing uncontrollably, until her cries were muted by an eerie hush and in that immediate quietness my thoughts gave birth to replaying the horrific accounts of what had transpired at Greg's condo, Monday night. I began reliving the moments when the officers turned on the lights in Greg's bedroom and there he was barely breathing and covered in blood and me beating a defenseless, heartless, romantic slayer.

My mind was certain that I had not caused that level of physical harm to Greg to warrant any sort of medical response.

Sure, I pummeled him about the face and head area, but not enough to cause any sort of medical triage. The amount of blood at the scene was horrific and incomprehensible. Greg's face was unrecognizable, and his body was completely covered by a blood-soaked sheet that I recall having many dalliances with Greg on, during happier days. I was certain I was not the perpetrator, but clearly someone else had a vendetta against Greg too and exacted their revenge on the same night I needed to confront him about destroying my life.

As I reached my prison cell, the corrections officer tugged my arm to alert me that I had reached my quarters. There I was standing in front of a jail cell that was now my new home. With that realization, I became extremely wobbly, and my feet felt as though they were nailed to the floor. The next thing I recalled was being dragged into my cell, pulled across the floor and slammed onto the hard, less than twin sized cot, equivalency. The tall, sturdy, middle-aged, female officer reminded me that if I continued to resist, it may affect my bail. The officer was a sister Queen. Her skin was a beautiful caramel color, and her eye whites were clear as day. "I'm warning you Ms. Ellison, if you continue to resist there will be harsh consequences that's a promise. Do I make myself clear?" She said in the sternest of tones I've ever heard since my formative years. I was still feeling very weak, and my vision for whatever reason was blurry at best. I had never been handled with such disrespect in all my life. I was mortified. In the feeblest of voices I asked, "Why am I being slammed around like a criminal? I've done nothing wrong", I added. The officer took offense to my appeal and walked over to the bunk that I was now laying on completely defenseless, squatted down next to me so that she and I were face to face and stated, "Ms. Ellison, contrary to what you might believe, you are a criminal. Just look at your blood-soaked hands! You may be somewhat privileged out there, but we enforce the law and maintain order here, and that applies to you. You might get away with beating up your boyfriend out there, but I strongly advise you not to press your luck in here. When I tell you to move, you move, or I may have to extend the right hand of fellowship to you, and I don't mean prayer. You got that?" She continued, "If you're nice to me, I'll be nice to you. Otherwise, there will be hell to pay in here for you. Ok, sweetie?" Before she could return to her standing position, I managed to read her name tag which read, "Officer Wahine." I began assuring the officer that I would never intentionally offend or disrespect her, but she brandished a wide smile, displaying a perfect set of teeth and said, "Too late, you already have." Officer Wahine returned to her standing position, winked at me, and then exited my cell.

The keys clanging against the bars sounded barbaric, scary, and final.

It was now Tuesday and given the amount of stress I had been dealing with I hadn't eaten well in four days, which may have accounted for why I'm feeling so weak. I was afraid to ask for anything to eat, because I didn't want any history of me spending time in such a facility, eating no less and besides, my family attorney would be returning soon, after posting bail.

I had determined to lay motionless, quietly listening to

my heart beating out of my chest, wondering if the little one inside of me was as terrified as I was. Everything was so surreal, and in an instant, everything about me had changed exponentially. I am pregnant. I am HIV positive. I am unemployed. I am afraid. I am disgraced. I am humiliated. I am incarcerated. It feels as if I am in an abyss and now everything is pitch-black, until I noticed a glimmer of light through my very blurry vision. It appears officer Wahine hadn't properly locked my cell door and it was slightly ajar. My first impression was to creep quietly towards the rusty bars and run my way to freedom, but I was too weak to even attempt such a feat. Instead, I laid there praying that my strength would return so that I could figure out the best way to escape. It was like magic, because within twenty minutes, miraculously, my strength and vision returned, and I was now up to the challenge. The atmosphere at the precinct was strangely quiet and officer Wahine was nowhere in sight.

With the perfect opportunity before me, I quickly made haste, gathered myself and quietly advanced towards the open cell door. I looked for the nearest exit and bolted in that direction to freedom. I exited a side door where there were several vehicles parked in the lot, but no staff. I was excited and afraid all at once, but remembered my assignment and continued to run until

I saw an oncoming delivery vehicle that slowed down as it approached me. I quickly asked the driver if I could use his cell phone to call my parents. The driver was an older gentleman and identified himself as Mr. Joe. As he handed me his phone, he asked me where I was going. I told him I was supposed to meet up with my parents but had lost my phone. Mr. Joe, peering over the top of his funny looking, broken glasses, said "I see." He went on to ask if my parents were expecting my call and I nodded yes. I made several attempts to reach my parents, but to no avail, so I left a voice message for my dad to pick me up at his office, which was in town and seemed to be a great meeting place. Mr. Joe asked me for the address to where I needed to be dropped off and then told me to hop in. Mr. Joe went on to add that he needed to make one final delivery, prior to giving me a ride to my destination. I agreed and happily climbed into his truck, where I felt a sense of complete calm and relief.

While we were en route to what was supposed to be Mr. Joe's last delivery, his demeanor was friendly and engaging. He said he had been in the delivery business for more than forty years and loved the flexibility that came with not being tied to a desk. At that time, I glanced at the back of his truck and noticed it was completely empty. When I turned back to look at Mr. Joe, by then he was looking at me out of the corner of his right eye, with his head still straight. Mr. Joe tapped his jacket pocket and said his last delivery was an envelope, as he had already delivered all the larger packages earlier on his route.

Before I could ask Mr. Joe to drop me off anywhere on his route, he picked up speed and stopped talking to me altogether. I asked him to please pull over, but he refused to look in my direction and I could see the blood coursing through the veins on the right side of his temple area. I began sobbing out of control and begged him to let me out and that's when he grabbed a handful of my hair and slammed my face into the dashboard, which left me dazed. Mr. Joe told me if I made one more sound it would be my last. Terrified, and with the vehicle still traveling at a high rate of speed, I leaped from the vehicle and rolled down an embankment screaming with every fiber of my being. Mr. Joe pulled the vehicle off the road and followed me down the embankment and proceeded to drag me back to his awaiting deathtrap. Bruised from the jump, and afraid for my life, I started kicking and punching Mr. Joe and began calling for help in my loudest voice, which is when Officer Wahine returned and demanded that I get up off the floor. She walked over to me and looked down on the floor at me and sternly advised me to stop the tantrums and disturbing outbursts, or I would find myself in solitary confinement until my lawyer posted bail. As I laid on the floor looking up at Officer Wahine, I was too exhausted from fighting off Mr. Joe, which was just another one of my crazy dreams, to defend myself and continued to sob quietly on my back until my lawyer returned hours later after posting bail and coordinating my release from jail.

I was escorted from jail, where my beloved mother emerged from my lawyer's vehicle, extremely emotional. My mother lovingly embraced me and assured me that no matter the outcome she would always love and support me. I assured her that I had not caused Greg the level of harm that I was being charged with and I would explain everything in its entirety. My attorney told me that I would need to appear in court in three days to learn the charges being levied against me. Since my condominium complex was still an active crime scene, I was advised by my attorney to avoid going back to my unit and to stay with my parents until further notice, but not before stopping by my attorney's office, so that he could take my statement regarding my account of what happened to Greg the night I was found striking him. Attorney Reynolds also stated that he needed to know every detail concerning my relationship with the victim.

The drive to my attorney's office was quiet. Upon arrival, we all entered his office, but my attorney requested that my parents remain outside in the waiting area until he was done taking my statement and going over the details of what transpired leading up to me being charged with aggravated assault and attempted murder. Attorney Reynolds, his assistant and I assembled ourselves in his very handsomely designed office, which is when he informed me that my parents had posted the five hundred thousand dollars cash bail needed to secure my release from jail. Attorney Reynolds also stated that if I fled or decided not to show up for my court appearance, my parents would lose the cash bail. I assured him that I would not do anything to jeopardize my parents' generosity nor waste his invaluable time defending me. With that, Attorney Reynolds asked me to start from the beginning regarding my relationship with Greg and requested specific details concerning how I ended up in the victim's condo unit covered in his blood.

I began from the beginning and shared all the details of my relationship with Greg. I also told him about the accounts leading up to the loss of my job, my pregnancy, and the fact that Greg had infected me with HIV. I went on to add that Greg was a serial cheater and had been cheating on me with men and women. I also admitted to vandalizing Greg's vehicle and leaving a hateful voice message on his phone, but I assured Attorney Reynolds that I had not seriously injured Greg. Attorney Reynolds' response to my account was stoic and professional. His assistant continued to transcribe and never flinched, even when the details of my account were less than glamorous. Attorney Reynolds advised me that it would be best if my parents heard the latest developments from me, rather than in court or in the media. I agreed and prepared myself mentally to talk with my parents.

After meeting with my legal team for what seemed like hours, my attorney ended the meeting by reminding me that I was not permitted to leave town, nor was I permitted to return to my condo, as it was still considered an active crime scene. I was also advised to refrain from speaking with anyone from the media. I agreed and as I exited his office, I signaled to my parents that I was ready to leave. As we were walking out of the building you could literally hear a pin drop and when my parents and I boarded my dad's vehicle my heart began racing at the very thought of sharing the shameful details of my sorted life, that at one point I had thoughts of bolting from the situation, running as fast as my legs could carry me in order to avoid having the much dreaded conversation with them, but instead, I steadied myself in the backseat, hung my head in shame and waited for my parents to start with the questions.

# Chapter 21

During the drive home my parents stopped by a local retail store to grab a few items for me, while I waited anxiously in the vehicle. Before exiting the vehicle, my mom turned to me and said she was running in the store to pick up a few items for me, since we couldn't return to my condo to get my things. I nodded in agreement, but never gave her any eye contact. After about thirty minutes in the store, my parents returned with several bags that they placed in the rear of the vehicle and my dad quietly commenced driving. We were about five minutes from my parents' house, when my dad, looking at me from the rearview mirror said, "Sweetheart, we are here for you, but we need for you to tell us how we got here. Dakota, we need the truth, and we need answers today. Your mom and I need to know what you're dealing with and how to prepare, mentally and financially to support you, but you must level with us." I began sobbing and apologized for the shame and hurt that I had caused them. By now we were in front of my parents' home, and I didn't want to leave the vehicle before sharing everything with them. I began explaining to them how I met Greg and all the details leading up to his betrayal. I told them about the text from his ex-fiancé and the incident in the parking lot where, I saw him kissing a man in the parking lot of our condominium complex.

I explained to my parents that Greg's double life and promiscuity scared me, which led me to visit the clinic to make sure I was ok. Before I could continue reliving the details, I began sobbing uncontrollably, but my parents' eyes were intentionally trained on me waiting for more information. After about ten seconds, I looked up at them both and blurted, "I am two months pregnant and also HIV positive." I went on to add that Greg isn't aware of my pregnancy or status, because he blocked my calls, because I lied to him about assisting him with processing his business loan application, which is why I went to his condo to let him know that he had infected me, and I was also carrying his child. I assured my parents that when I arrived at Greg's unit, the door was already open, the lighting was low, and Greg was lying in bed already injured. I further admitted to them that I began hitting Greg for blocking my calls, jeopardizing my job and for infecting me with HIV and that's when the police arrived to find him unresponsive and me standing over him with his blood on my clothing and hands. With that revelation, my parents were surprisingly quiet and asked if Greg was the only gentleman that I had been seeing. I assured my parents that I don't sleep around, and Greg was the only person that I had known intimately in many, many months and there wasn't any other gentleman in my life. My mom gently took my hand in hers and said, "Dakota, I am so very sorry you are in this predicament, but we are here for you and will address everything that you are faced with as a family. Dakota, you are loved and have a support system. You also need to know that you can come to us with anything." Before my mom could say anything more, my dad exited the vehicle, opened the rear door, and began hugging me and sobbing quietly. I broke down in my daddy's arms, because finally I felt I didn't have to carry everything I was feeling, alone. I closed my eyes and allowed my dad's strong arms to pull me in. I felt protected, safe, but more importantly loved. My dad whispered in my ear, "You will always be my baby girl, so don't ever feel alone in this world. Kota, I will go to the end of the world for you, because I'm your father." My dad proceeded to kiss my forehead and lovingly walked me into the house and escorted me to my old bedroom. He smiled at me and said, "You're home now." I gave my dad the biggest hug and told him how much I loved him and entered my room for some much-needed rest, but not before visiting the kitchen for a good meal, of course.

# Chapter 22

Staying at my parent's house was amazing. The neighborhood was perfect in every way and my parents never made my situation, condition, or status a daily topic of discussion. Instead, they provided me with the space to share at my leisure. I was starting to feel like my old self again, until I realized I was still HIV positive, pregnant, and needed prenatal and medical follow up. Therefore, I placed a call to the clinic to schedule a follow up appointment for the following week, as I was ending my call with the clinic, my phone rang and it was my Attorney, calling to inform me that we needed to meet to discuss several important latest developments pertaining to my case. I agreed to meet with him as soon as possible. Therefore, he agreed to meet with me later in the day at 4:30 p.m., at his office. I ended the call and immediately joined my mom in the kitchen where I explained to her that I needed to meet with Attorney Reynolds today at 4:30 p.m. My mom nodded in agreement, and we left two hours later to get ahead of the rush hour traffic so that we would arrive in ample time for my meeting. The drive to the office was upbeat and fun. Mom and I chatted about the beautiful, sundrenched day and how the day was perfect for a long drive.

We arrived at my attorney's office at 4:10 p.m. Attorney Reynolds was expecting us and greeted us as we entered the office. He and my mom exchanged niceties and then he and I headed into the conference room. I noticed his assistant wasn't present, so I took that as a good sign. Attorney Reynolds immediately started with, "Dakota, you look great. How have you been doing since I last saw you?" I told him I was doing fine, and I had earlier in the day scheduled an appointment to see my Dr. for the upcoming week. He then replied, "That's great. I'm happy you are continuing to take care of yourself and the baby." I smiled and then sat up in my chair to hear the latest update regarding my case and more importantly Greg. Attorney Reynolds continued, "Dakota, you should be the first to know that all the charges against you have been dropped. Greg is doing remarkably well now and was able to identify the individuals that assaulted him. I am not at liberty to share that information with you, but you are free to return to your condo, without incident. Greg has asked that the charges against you be completely dropped and has refused to participate in any legal proceedings against you. However, from a legal perspective, for right now, I strongly urge you to stay away from Greg and his condo unit, because the next time you may not be as lucky." He continued, "On another note, Greg is aware of your condition and knows that you are expecting. However, concerning your HIV status, Greg has been tested on three separate occasions and has tested negative. Therefore, you did not contract HIV from Greg, nor is it clear how or from whom you obtained your HIV status." With that information, I was left speechless, mortified, stunned, and scared. Attorney Reynolds words were stern as he concluded, "Dakota, respectfully, you need to make every effort to recall your male suitors and if Greg is found to be the father of your unborn child, then you need to interact with him at some point, but only if you can handle yourself in a mature and respectful manner. Otherwise, you may find yourself here again. Does that make sense?" I shook my head in agreement but couldn't believe what I was hearing. Greg had tested negative for HIV and had requested that all charges against me be dropped.

I asked Attorney Reynolds if he had spoken to my parents regarding this latest development. He assured me that he was bound by the attorney-client privilege which prevents him from discussing or disclosing anything from our meetings with anyone. Attorney Reynolds stated that it was up to me if I wanted to share the details from the meeting with my parents. I thanked him for the information and exited the office. I joined my mom, who was anxiously waiting for me. I hugged her and told her that the charges had been dropped, as Greg was doing well and had identified his perpetrators. My mom began sobbing uncontrollably and thanking God out loud. I should have been happier, but I wasn't, because I still hadn't told my mom about Greg's negative HIV status. I guess I wasn't ready for her double disappointment and the questions that would follow. My mom quickly called my dad and gave him the update and I could hear my father breathing a sigh of relief through the phone. My mom tried passing the phone to me, but I pretended to be in a hurry to leave the office and refused to take the phone. My mom told my dad we were leaving the office and would call him from the car.

During the drive home, my mom asked if there was something more that I hadn't shared with her, because I seemed distant. I told her that I was still in shock from everything and just needed to take it all in. I also told her that I had scheduled a follow up appointment at the clinic for the coming week and needed to stay focused on that. My mother said the worst was over and I had her full support. She further added that she would drive me to my appointments and was willing to learn more about the whole HIV disease so that we could address it as a family, especially with the baby coming. I thanked her for her support and told her I would take it one day at a time.

The drive home was different. My mom played her favorite gospel music the entire time, while I was still focused on Greg. I felt he genuinely cared about me to request to have all criminal charges against me dropped, even after I deceived him with the loan application thingy, vandalized his vehicle and was also found in his condo assaulting him, while he lay injured. In that moment I determined I needed to see him. When we returned home, my dad was there with dinner that he had brought in. My dad was so relieved that I wouldn't be tried criminally and all charges against me would be expunged. My parents were so jubilant that I wasn't sure if telling them about Greg's status was important or even relevant anymore. I didn't want them to think I was a loose woman, or irresponsible. Therefore, I decided not to tell them. I didn't want to ruin the evening. I decided to turn in around 10:30 p.m., even though I wasn't tired. I just needed to be alone.

# Chapter 23

That night I laid in bed all night thinking about how I might have contracted HIV, but mostly about Greg and how I needed to see him to apologize for everything and to discuss our unborn child. Since I couldn't sleep, at around 7:30 a.m. I decided to get up, dress and ask my parents to drop me back at my condo. I exited my room and waited quietly in the kitchen. My dad entered the kitchen around 8:30 a.m. and said, "Hey Kid, I see you're up early this morning. What's up?" I looked at my dad with a half-smile and a disingenuous giggle and said, "Nothing. I just thought I would get an early start and head back home." My dad, looking over his glasses said, "Are you sure?"

I nodded yes and he, in the most chipper voice said, "Ok, let me get some clothes on and I'll take you home." My dad gave me a wink with his right eye and exited the kitchen to get dressed. My mom entered the kitchen and said she was happy I was returning home but warned me to be careful and if I needed to come back home for any reason the door would always be open. I thanked my mom and gave her the biggest hug, ever.

During the commute home dad asked if I needed him to walk me up to my unit. I said yes, because I wasn't sure what to expect, especially since my condo unit was part of the crime scene, concerning Greg's assault. When we arrived, the complex parking lot appeared normal, but I didn't see Greg's vehicle. My dad escorted me up to my condo and to our surprise everything was exactly as I had left it. My dad turned to me and said, "You know you dodged a bullet, right?" In a sigh of relief, I nodded in agreement and just held his strong hand in mine. My dad walked me through the entire unit and then said he needed to leave but was only a phone call away if I needed him. He gave me a kiss on the forehead and exited my condo to start his day. It was strange being back home after being paraded through the lobby in handcuffs, the night Greg was assaulted, but I needed to get back into my normal rhythm. Since this whole ordeal, I hadn't checked my email, text messages or social media accounts. I was too afraid. Therefore, I sat down and began looking through my text messages and saw a barrage of incoming messages and began responding back to each of them until I drifted off to sleep. A few hours later, I awoke to slight cramping in my stomach, attributed it to gas, especially since my eating was completely thrown off. I got a quick bite, showered, and decided to go for a walk around the reservoir. I completed the walk and returned to the condominium complex where everything seemed normal. I called my parents to let them know I was ok and would be turning in for the night.

I spent the next few days by myself but adjusting to my new normal. My belly was starting to stick out a bit and I was feeling extremely tired. I reached out to my girls to see if we could get together for a quick bite, but only one person responded, and she said she was busy. I guess they were feeling put off by me dropping out of site for weeks and not keeping in touch. Therefore, I sent them another text apologizing for my disappearing act and explaining to them that I needed to connect with them to explain everything. After sending the text message, the cramping in my belly returned with a vengeance and after going to the bathroom I noticed I was also spotting. I immediately called the clinic and was advised to come in immediately, even though my scheduled appointment was only two days away. I drove myself to the clinic, secured parking and entered the Dr.'s office. Upon my arrival, I was processed by the front desk associate and called in to see the Dr., immediately after. My physician triaged my condition and sent me down for a pelvic ultrasound to see if I there were any problems with my pregnancy. After the procedure I returned to the examination room, where I was informed that I was experiencing a miscarriage. The Dr. told me that this usually occurs within the first trimester and is a signal that there are viability issues with the fetus.

The nurse provided me with specific information pertaining to my immediate situation and told me to come back in two days for my scheduled appointment to discuss my HIV status and medication protocol.

As I exited the clinic, I was too shocked to cry or be upset. "What else?" I screamed in the parking lot. I drove home and never shed a tear. I was so proud of myself, for not having an anxiety attack and going crazy in my head. On another note, my mom was a prayer warrior, and I was forever in her prayers and now I was reaping the benefits from all of her hard work, because God knows my prayer life was nowhere in sight. I felt a sense of peace and calm.

For the first time I didn't feel alone. I felt ok with dealing with my situation rationally. When I returned home, I was still cramping and bleeding, but I was prepared with what to expect and pushed through it. I didn't bother phoning my parents, I figured I would call them after my appointment in two days.

The day of my scheduled Dr.'s appointment happened upon me in the blink of an eye. The appointment went well. They ordered a battery of blood work, explained the medication that I would have to take and suggested I join an HIV support group, so that I could learn more about the disease and meet others who are successfully thriving while living with the disease.

The nurse handed me written instructions for taking my pharmaceuticals and said she would call in my prescription to my usual pharmacy. I agreed and said I would consider joining the support group, even though that was a lie. I left the clinic, ran a few errands, picked up my medication and headed home. As I entered the lobby, I headed towards the elevator, but not before stopping to collect my mail from my mailbox. I pressed the elevator button and after about twenty seconds, the elevator arrived and I proceeded to press the button to advance to the tenth floor, my floor. I arrived at my unit but could not get my mind off Greg and who was responsible for assaulting him. I also wondered if he was home or still in the hospital. I quickly dismissed Greg from my mind because I had my own immediate concerns to deal with. I was miscarrying his child. I was now on HIV medication and although I was being paid during my suspension through my accrued vacation and compensation time, I was still very much unemployed, which was a good thing given all the *shiggady* going on in my life. Not to mention, I still desperately needed to find out how I contracted HIV, which was too painful for me to begin to figure out.

Weeks went by and oddly enough my parents respectfully allowed me to grow in my new normal with little to no interference. I hadn't told my parents or Greg about the miscarriage and therefore decided it was time. I called my mom, and she picked up on the second ring and said, "Hi Baby! How are you doing?" I told her I was as well as could be expected and told her I had something to share with her. She assured me she was all ears. I commenced telling her that I was no longer pregnant, as I had suffered a miscarriage a few weeks back. My mom was strangely quiet. "Mom are you there?" I asked. "Yes, baby, I'm here. I'm sorry you had to go through that alone." She responded. She further asked, "Why didn't you call me, sweetie?" I told her that I was doing well, and I didn't feel the need to call anyone, because for the first time in my life I didn't feel afraid to face anything. I told her she could tell dad and that I was doing well and had already started taking my HIV medication and was adjusting to my new normal. My mom said she was proud of me and assured me that if I needed anything to give her a call, but not before telling me she loved me.

Even though my mom's behavior was a bit odd, I was proud of myself for handling that call so well. I then felt the urge to level with Greg, to apologize to him for my behavior towards him, to also thank him for dropping the charges against me and lastly to let him know that I am no longer pregnant with his child. In the spirit of doing the right thing, I located Greg's number in my phone and called him and to my surprise the phone rang. Greg had unblocked my number. My heart almost jumped out of my chest, and I almost hung up, when I heard his voice on the other end, "Hi Dakota. I knew you would eventually call.," Greg said. Nervously, and softly I replied, "Hi Greg. How are you doing? I won't keep you long, but I just wanted to first and foremost apologize for my behavior towards you, including the deception concerning your loan application. Please forgive me." To savor the moment, I started my audio recorder on my phone and continued,

"Greg, I also wanted to thank you for extending grace and not pressing charges against me. I am deeply grateful to you for that." Greg sighed aloud and said, "You're forgiven. Dakota, I heard you're pregnant. Is that true? I also heard that you are HIV positive, is that true? My gut instinct was to lie, but I was tired of pretending, so I admitted to being pregnant, but told him I subsequently miscarried, but yes, I was diagnosed with HIV when all the crazy stuff happened. Before I could say anything more, Greg interjected, "Dakota, I am HIV negative, and I am unable to have children due to my very low testosterone count. I've known this for years, which is why I was extremely crushed when I learned about the paternity ordeal with my ex. The detectives pressed me about my involvements when I was assaulted and that's when I admitted that I am bisexual and wasn't necessarily open about it. However, I want you to know that if you were pregnant, it couldn't have been mine. I am not able to father children, because I suffer with azoospermia, a condition where I have a zero sperm count. When I heard you were pregnant, it was DeJa'Vu all over again for me." I couldn't believe what I was hearing. "If I wasn't pregnant by Greg, then who?" I said to myself. I hadn't been involved with anyone while I was seeing Greg. In a frenzy I assured Greg that I had not been intimately involved with anyone and couldn't understand what he was saying. Maybe the sperm count levels had returned because none of what he was saying made sense.

Greg, continued, "Dakota, why haven't you asked me who assaulted me the night you were found in my condo, or do you already know?" Even more confused I asked, "Greg, what do you mean? I honestly have no idea who would have wanted to cause you harm. The only reason I was so upset with you is because you jeopardized my job, and when I saw you in the parking lot kissing that guy, I was shocked. And before that, I also read the text message from your ex regarding the two of you hooking up while you were seeing me. I was confused and afraid. And then when I learned I was pregnant and HIV positive, I thought it was you who infected me. I panicked and went nuts, especially when I couldn't reach you and later learned you had blocked my number and refused to take my calls. Please tell me who injured you and why would you think I would know?" Greg, in the most quiet and sinister voice said, "Go ask your father. Your father isn't the man who he claims to be, or you perceive him to be. Your dad is the king of the closet. If I pursued the legal realm against you, I would have disappeared without a trace. But now I am no longer afraid of him and his minions. Yeah, go ask him, maybe he can explain everything. According to the medical professionals, I was left for dead and you storming into my condo and smacking me around saved my life, because the neighbors heard the noise and called the police. So, I guess I am indebted to you for saving my life. Otherwise, I would have been there for days and eventually have succumbed to my injuries." Greg continued, "Dakota, the unit that I occupy is not mine, it is owned by your father, and I stay here, because that's the least he could do, given the years we have been involved with each other as business partners, but more as partners and zero business. I only involved you to get his attention and boy did I ever get his attention." Greg continued his rant, "The gloves are off now, and I am no longer going to keep his little secret, especially after he nearly took my life." Greg's tone became cold and resolute. Nervously, I asked, "Greg, are you trying to tell me that you were with me and my dad at the same time?" Greg's response was coupled with a menacing chuckle as he mercilessly blurted out, "Go ask your father." And then abruptly ended the call. I immediately saved the audio recording from our conversation and listened to it again to make sure I clearly understood what Greg had just admitted to. Mortified, I tried calling Greg back, but he wouldn't answer, but at least he hadn't blocked my number.

# Chapter 24

I couldn't believe what Greg was saying about him and my dad, so I immediately called my father, but he didn't answer so I left a very calm message requesting a call back. I wanted to hear my father's side of the story before calling my mother, but I couldn't reach her either. I asked her to call me back and was sure to remain as calm as possible while leaving my message. I tried calling Greg again, and he answered the phone, but left the line open so that I could hear him and another gentleman in the background having a verbal exchange. I instantly began recording the audio from the call, just to cover myself and in case Greg was found hurt again. Greg was telling the person that the relationship was over and the love he once had for him was gone. I then heard Greg specifically call the gentleman by his surname, Mr. Ellison. MY DAD!! I was now listening to a lovers spat between my dad and Greg, my boyfriend. My dad could be heard professing his feelings to Greg and telling him that he would do anything to keep him in his life, and how he needed more time to sort things out in his marriage. Greg told my dad that he would continue to date other people as long as my dad was still living with his wife and a married man. My dad told Greg that he didn't have a problem with him seeing other people but warned him that if he continued to pursue me, he wouldn't be responsible for his actions. After that exchange there was some mumbling and then the talking completely stopped. I then heard what sounded like intimate exchanges, with groaning and sighs and that's when I had heard enough and purposely ended the call.

After about ten minutes I called my dad's phone again and he didn't answer. I then gathered my keys and headed to the parking lot, where I found my dad's vehicle parked in a very clandestine area, but on the premises, nonetheless. I called my dad's phone again and he answered, he seemed out of breath and asked if I was ok. I told him I was fine and asked him if he was in the area, he said he was at the gym, but would swing by if I needed anything. Shocked by his blatant lie, I told him I was fine and was looking for mom. He said he hadn't spoken with her in a couple of hours but was sure she was probably out with friends. He hurried me off the phone and said he had to get back to his workout and would call me in about an hour, or so. I took a picture of his vehicle and parked my vehicle clear across the lot, but within view of his vehicle. My father did not emerge from Greg's condo for another three hours, which was well into the evening. I was sure to video tape him walking across the lot and driving out of the parking lot. I immediately called my mom again and she answered the phone, very groggy. She said she had been napping all evening and had just gotten up when she heard the phone. I asked her if she was feeling ok, and she said she was fine. She said she recalled having a light lunch with dad and then immediately after she drifted off to sleep. I asked her if dad was at home, and she said he had a late business meeting concerning a new project across town and wouldn't be back home until around 10:00 p.m. As we were on the phone talking my mother said my dad was calling her on the other line, so she would need to call me right back and our call ended. I called Greg back and he didn't answer, so I decided to call it a night and address everything in the morning. And out of respect for my mother I vowed to never speak to Greg again and to tell my mother about my father's double life.

# Chapter 25

I hadn't seriously prayed in years, but that night before retiring for the evening, I said a prayer for me and my family. I hadn't prayed for a long time, but I desperately needed God's help, because nothing seemed ok anymore and I needed guidance. My father was a very powerful developer in the area and if his situation was made public, the scandal would not only destroy him, but also my mother and the entire family. My father was a well-respected developer and real estate tycoon and revered by many as an upstanding employer in the North Carolina area. Any news of his infidelity would result in a huge exposé. After praying I drifted off to sleep and slept like a baby.

When I awoke in the morning it was about 7:40 a.m. and the sun was gracing my bedroom on that beautiful morning. I quickly checked my phone to see if mom had called me back, from the night before, but she hadn't. However, I did notice an email message from my manager. The message stated that my suspension had been lifted and the incident was expunged from my employment record. My manager further stated in the communication that my vacation time and compensation time would be made whole, and I would have those balances restored. Basically, I had been suspended with pay. She went on to add that I could report to work on Monday, full-time. I quickly responded and told her that I would see her on Monday. I called my mother, and she answered on the first ring. "Good morning sweetie! How are you doing this morning?" She said in the most chipper voice. I told her I was fine and began filling her in on the details of my job. I told her that all my accrued time was being restored and the whole incident with Greg had been expunged from my employment record. Mom was super excited and began thanking God. I went on to tell her that I had prayed the night before and would continue praying for our family. My mother was overjoyed that I was talking about prayer and told me that God answers prayers and therefore, I was on the right track.

I asked her if dad was still asleep, and she said he was in the shower preparing for his day. Mom chuckled admiringly and said that dad arrived home around 11:15 p.m. the night before and spent the entire night working late in his study and eventually fell asleep while working. I could hear my father in the background and my mother left the phone briefly to update him regarding my job. I then heard my father's voice on the phone saying, "Hey Kid, how are you this morning? Congratulations. It's nice to know that you will be heading back to work next week." "Thank you, dad. Yes, it will be nice to return to work and to have things return to normal.," I replied. My father said he would catch up with me later and then handed the phone back to my mother. My mother asked what my plans were for the day, and I told her I needed to talk with her about an important matter and invited her to lunch. She insisted I come to the house and promised she would make my favorite chickpea salad. Since that was one of my favorite foods, I agreed and told her I would be there around noon. When we ended the call I prayed again, asking God to give me the words to say to my mother regarding the latest revelation concerning my father's double life.

I showered and headed out to have lunch with my mom. The

drive to my parents' home was glorious and I arrived at 11:30 a.m. When I arrived, my mom was home alone. Therefore, I rang the bell and entered with my key. My mom was thrilled that we were going to spend the day together and could barely contain herself. She thought I wanted to talk about my status, but I assured her that I was doing well and taking my medication faithfully. I wasn't hungry and decided it would be best to have the talk with my mother well in advance of my father returning home. Therefore, I asked my mother what time my dad would be arriving back home. My mother assured me that dad would be gone all day and wasn't expected back home until 8 p.m. I immediately brought my mother into the kitchen, and I told her I loved her and only wanted what was best for her. As I fought for the words to start the delicate conversation, I could see the concern in her face and before I could continue, my phone continued to vibrate incessantly out of control. I asked my mother to excuse me for a moment while I retrieved my phone from my purse and that's when I saw four consecutive text messages from Greg, which read, "Your dad is looking for you. He knows that you are aware of his double life. He was here earlier and saw my call log. He knows I called you when he was in my condo last night. He left here quite angry, so please be careful." I turned to my mother and told her we needed to leave, but noticed she was on the phone talking with my dad. She had a very peculiar look on her face and told my dad not to worry, she would wait for him. I convinced my mother that we wouldn't be long and begged her to take the ride with me. After much pleading she agreed to take a small drive with me but made me promise to have her back home in time to meet up with my dad. I assured her we wouldn't be gone for very long. She then hurried off to gather her things so we could have a quiet place to chat. Besides, my mom needed to see my dad for who he really is, and she also needed to listen to the audio from my dad's intimate encounter with Greg.

My mom is an amazing, honest person and she deserves to know the truth.

My mom and I quickly hopped into my car, and I drove to the furthest body of water to chat. I always felt that being near the ocean water in many ways is therapeutic, nurturing and healing. I found the perfect parking spot and began nervously explaining to my mom why I asked her to meet with me. I told her about Greg's assault and who was behind it and why. I also told her about dad's double life and how he had been intimately involved with the same guy I was dating. I went on to tell her that Greg started dating me to force dad's hand in ending his marriage and that's when dad had him roughed up and severely injured. My mother began screaming at me and telling me I'm out of my mind and my dad would never hurt anyone or do anything to hurt their marriage. My mother further stated, "Dakoata, this is none of your business, but your dad has been suffering with erectile dysfunction for the past ten years and has been completely unable to perform sexually. I stayed with him, because I love him, and my love extends beyond the lack of intimacy. So, you see, your dad is incapable of engaging in any extramarital affairs, because it's physically impossible for him to do so. Besides, I have never had any woman call my house looking for your dad, nor has any woman ever accused your father of being anything but respectful. Baby Girl, you've been through a lot over the past couple of months, so you're probably hyper emotional right now, but what you're saying doesn't make any sense, given your dad's medical circumstance."

In shock, I took her by the hand and explained to her that dad had been deceiving her and I needed her to listen to something. I immediately retrieved my phone and played the audio version of his romantic interlude with Greg. When we were done listening to that audio clip, I played the other audio clip from my earlier conversation with Greg, where he was explicit in explaining that my father wasn't who I thought he was. Finally, I showed her the text message from Greg, where Greg stated that my dad was aware that I knew about the two of them. My mom turned to me and asked me to take her home. There wasn't a tear in her eye during the entire drive home. The drive home was somber. I begged my mother not to immediately confront my dad. I told her I didn't want things to get out of control and was afraid things could escalate quickly, especially given the level of betrayal. My mom turned to me and said, "You have enough of your own personal stuff to tend to, so don't worry about me. I got this. All I need you to do is send me both audio clips and the text message." I pulled over and forwarded the audio clips and text messages and continued our commute.

As we approached my parents' house, my dad's vehicle was clearly visible in the driveway, and he could be seen pacing back and forth on the front porch. As we pulled in the driveway behind my dad's vehicle, my mom was the first one to exit the vehicle and began walking towards my dad. My dad was now face to face with my mom, when suddenly, my mom blurted out, "So, you like men, huh? You've been lying to me for years about your impotence and erectile dysfunction issues, but it was all a lie. Mr. Ellison, who are you? What kind of monster deceives his wife for years, while living on the downlow?" My dad just stood there, total devoid of any words. My mom continued, "I sent you a little something I think you should listen to." But before my dad could respond, my mom began playing the clip of his romantic interlude with Greg, on her phone, right in the driveway. My dad was frozen after listening to the clip, at which time he turned around and started heading back into the house, but before he could reach the stairs he collapsed and hit his head on the concrete steps.

My mom began demanding that he get up. Thinking he tripped I ran over to assist and realized my dad was unconscious and totally unresponsive. I immediately called 911 and the paramedics arrived within minutes.

# About the Author

**Sharon Butler-Charles** is a fourth time author who successfully published her first adult abstract poetry book entitled, "Soliloquy Chasms of the Mind," two Children's books entitled, "Nippy Neire & Mr. Butterfly" and "The Daily Adventures of ZuLu" and now her fourth book entitled, "The Daily Chronicles of Dakota Ellison."

**The Daily Chronicles of Dakota Ellison** is a two-part adult novella that depicts a young Nubian, African American professional female who has been dealing with salacious recuring nightmares and daydreams that leave her cerebrally exhausted and often unable to separate reality from her illusive perceptions, as it relates to her intimate entanglements.

Dakota's inability to safely navigate her life rationally leads her down a dark path that derails her life professionally, ethically, morally, and mentally.

This Novella is a fiction-based, romance-thriller that is dripping with fantasy, passion, mystery, suspense, and gut-wrenching dalliances that push the envelope of sanity to the point of no return.

**Sharon Butler-Charles** is a native Bostonian and the proud mother of two of two adult children. Prior to embarking on her writing endeavors, she successfully earned an undergraduate degree in business administration and a master's degree in organizational leadership – (Non-Profit). Sharon has a passion for writing and has more writing projects in the pipeline.